H. E. Bates was born in 1905 at Rushden in Northampton-
shire and was educated at Kettering Grammar School. He
worked as a journalist and clerk on a local newspaper before
publishing his first book, *The Two Sisters*, when he was
twenty. In the next fifteen years he acquired a distinguished
reputation for his stories about English country life. During
the Second World War, he was a Squadron Leader in the
R.A.F. and some of his stories of service life, *The Greatest
People in the World* (1942), *How Sleep the Brave* (1943) and
The Face of England (1953), were written under the pseu-
donym of 'Flying Officer X'. His subsequent novels of
Burma, *The Purple Plain* and *The Jacaranda Tree*, and of
India, *The Scarlet Sword*, stemmed directly or indirectly
from his war experience in the Eastern theatre of war.

In 1958 his writing took a new direction with the appearance
of *The Darling Buds of May*, the first of the popular Larkin
family novels, which was followed by *A Breath of French
Air*, *When the Green Woods Laugh*, *Oh! To Be in England*, and
A Little of What You Fancy. The Larkin sequence is published
in Penguin in one volume entitled *Perfick, Perfick!* His
autobiography appeared in three volumes, *The Vanished
World* (1969), *The Blossoming World* (1971) and *The World in
Ripeness* (1972). His last works included the novel *The
Triple Echo* (1971) and a collection of short stories, *The Song
of the Wren* (1972). Perhaps one of his most famous works
of fiction is the best-selling novel *Fair Stood the Wind for
France* (1944). H. E. Bates also wrote miscellaneous works
on gardening, essays on country life, several plays including
The Day of Glory (1945), *The Modern Short Story* (1941) and
a story for children, *The White Admiral* (1968). His works
have been translated into sixteen languages and a posthum-
ous collection of his stories, *The Yellow Meads of Asphodel*,
appeared in 1976.

H. E. Bates was awarded the C.B.E. in 1973 and died in
January 1974. He was married in 1931 and had four children.

H. E. BATES

The Fabulous Mrs V.

PENGUIN BOOKS

PENGUIN BOOKS

Published by the Penguin Group
27 Wrights Lane, London W8 5TZ, England
Viking Penguin Inc., 40 West 23rd Street, New York, New York 10010, USA
Penguin Books Australia Ltd, Ringwood, Victoria, Australia
Penguin Books Canada Ltd, 2801 John Street, Markham, Ontario, Canada L3R 1B4
Penguin Books (NZ) Ltd, 182–190 Wairau Road, Auckland 10, New Zealand

Penguin Books Ltd, Registered Offices: Harmondsworth, Middlesex, England

First published by Michael Joseph 1964
Published in Penguin Books 1970
5 7 9 10 8 6 4

Copyright © Evensford Productions Ltd, 1964
All rights reserved

Made and printed in Great Britain by
Hazell Watson & Viney Limited
Member of BPCC Limited
Aylesbury, Bucks, England
Set in Linotype Pilgrim

Except in the United States of America,
this book is sold subject to the condition
that it shall not, by way of trade or otherwise,
be lent, re-sold, hired out, or otherwise circulated
without the publisher's prior consent in any form of
binding or cover other than that in which it is
published and without a similar condition
including this condition being imposed
on the subsequent purchaser

Contents

And No Birds Sing

IT wasn't only being alone; it was the way the house smelt dead.

She sat under a big sweet-chestnut tree, in the heart of the woodland, watching Mr Thompson with grave brown eyes. Mr Thompson was frying mushrooms over a hazel fire in an old half-circular billy-can. The peculiar aroma of hazel smoke and the tang of mushrooms was so strong on the October evening air that every now and then she licked her lips like someone in a hungry dream.

'Never had wild mushrooms before,' she said. 'Never knew you could get them wild.'

'No?' Mr Thompson said. He kept turning the mushrooms over with the point of an old bone-handled shut knife. 'And how old did you say you was?'

'Twelve.'

'Don't they tell you nothing at school?'

'Not about mushrooms.'

'The sort you git in shops eat like leather,' Mr Thompson said. He dropped another lump of butter into the mushrooms. The butter sizzled and he lifted the billy-can a few inches off the fire. 'Don't taste of nothing at all.'

'I only ever had them out of tins.'

'Tins, eh?' Mr Thompson said. 'They git 'em up in tins now, do they?'

Mr Thompson took the billy-can completely off the fire and peered down at the mushrooms. The girl sat holding an egg in each hand. Something about the neutral blankness of the eggs seemed to be reflected in her eyes and she hardly stirred as Mr Thompson took the eggs away from her and broke them one by one into a battered coffee tin.

'Smells rich,' she said.

Mr Thompson beat the eggs with his knife. His face was rough and greyish from a two-day growth of beard. The battered brown hat that was pushed to the back of his head made his eyes appear to be protuberant, like a pair of big blue marbles, but at the same time docile, harmless and contented.

'It's quiet in the wood tonight,' she said. 'You don't even hear the birds.'

'No, the birds are settling down. I heard an old pheasant a little while back though.'

'Pheasant? Are they wild too?'

'Sort of,' Mr Thompson said. 'Half an' half, this time o' year. Half-wild, half-tame. Till they git shot at a bit.'

'Tame? You mean you could keep one in a cage? Like a budgie?'

'No,' Mr Thompson said. He laughed. 'They ain't them sort o' birds.'

She sat quiet, her eyes roving to and fro suddenly, half-wild, half-tame themselves. The birds, like the mushrooms, were another part of her many revelations. Their songs woke her in the early mornings, before the mists cleared, when she sometimes lay alone for a long time under Mr Thompson's raincoat, staring up at the great roof of branches, wondering if Mr Thompson had gone away and left her. This was the time of day when she remembered most clearly the way the house smelt: that dead smell, the smell of night before day washed it away.

But before very long Mr Thompson was always back, bringing mushrooms, blackberries, wood-nuts, perhaps a bit of watercress, clean water for her to wash in and fresh branches for the fire. Once he brought a handful of wheat-ears and the sound of them being rubbed between the leathery palms of his hands was the sound that woke her.

'Mum works at the food factory,' she said. 'I told you that though, didn't I? She brings stuff home. I think she wins it – you know. That's how I know about the mushrooms that one time.'

'Wins it?'

'Bones it. You know.'

'Works too, does she? All day?'

'All day. She'd work all night too if they'd let her. Wants to get the fridge paid off. The telly took two years. She wants a spin dryer next. She's gone before eight in the morning and gets back about ten at night. Does a washing-up job at a hotel on the way back. That's what makes her bad tempered.'

That too was why the house smelt dead. You didn't really live in it and it just smelt dead. It was a hole you crawled back to after work was over. Her father was away at half-past six in the morning and sometimes in the winter she didn't see him at all. With overtime he was knocking up big money. They were both knocking it up. Really big. All the time.

Mr Thompson, giving the beaten eggs a screw of salt, poured them into the billy-can with the mushrooms and started to scramble them with his knife, holding the can at the very edge of the fire.

'Hand us that spoon, will you?' he said. 'And you cut some bread with my knife. We'll be ready in a minute now.'

She started to cut slices of bread from a loaf. The aroma of eggs scrambled in with mushrooms rose more richly than ever through the woodland air. Everything Mr Thompson cooked was good. Everything that had happened with Mr Thompson was good. Everything since she had first met him on her way home from school five days ago had been good. It was all a revelation.

'You can have the spoon back now. I'll eat mine with me knife.'

The only utensils Mr Thompson seemed to possess were the spoon, the knife, the billy-can, the coffee tin, a cup, an old blue plate and a kettle. Now he put half the scrambled eggs and mushrooms on the plate and the kettle on the fire.

'Eat up,' Mr Thompson said. 'It gits cold quick out here.'

She started shovelling eggs and mushrooms into her mouth with the spoon, cramming slices of bread in after them like wads of stuffing. Her own eyes were protuberant now : big with unconscious, happy greed. Small points of reflected firelight gave them excitement too, so that she might have been sitting there watching some complex sort of drama being played out on a screen.

While she was cramming in the food Mr Thompson paused in his eating to wash out the old coffee tin with boiling water. Then

he dropped a handful of tea and sugar and half a tin of con-
densed milk into the kettle and stirred it round several times
with a hazel stick, finally letting it all boil up.

Even the smell of tea excited her. Like everything else it was
good too. It was good and living. Lost and rapturous, she sat
there eating madly, waiting for her cup to come.

'Been holding your cup out a good minute,' Mr Thompson
said. 'Don't you want it? Been thinking of something?'

She didn't say anything; she didn't tell Mr Thompson how,
for quite five minutes, she had been thinking again of the dead
smell of home and how it seemed to strangle her: the living-
room with the telly, the fridge, the radio, the cooker and the
washing machine all crammed in together, the table with un-
cleared breakfast remains still on it when she got back from
school, the grey eye of the television set holding her a mute
captive there in the dead half-darkness while she waited for
someone to come home.

She merely said instead: 'I was thinking how you're always
so friendly.'

'Got nothing to be unfriendly about. Got nobody to quarrel
with.'

She gulped fast at her cup of tea, staring at him with big grave
eyes over the top of it. She was right about Mr Thompson: he
was always so quiet and friendly – like the day she first ran
into him, carrying his bundle of utensils, his raincoat and two
loaves of bread. It was because he accidentally dropped one of
the loaves and she picked it up for him that they got talking and
finally walked on together. That was the first time she was
struck by the large, friendly eyes.

She had never really been aware of how far they walked that
first afternoon; perhaps it wasn't all that far. But because Mr
Thompson walked slowly, unprepossessed by time or distance,
it seemed a long way. In an hour they were in the woods and
Mr Thompson was saying:

'You'd better git back now, hadn't you?'

She remembered that moment very well. She knew for an
awful certainty that she wasn't going back. She remembered a
shadow of sickness falling on her as her thoughts went back to

the living-room and in a moment the stranglehold of it was round her neck.

She begged Mr Thompson to let her stay a little longer and he said:

'Well, I'm going to boil myself a drop o' tea. You better have a cup before you go.'

After that, as she did now, she sat watching him over the top of the tea cup. The shadows of late afternoon fell on his face, breaking it up into a benign and trembling pattern, and she knew for the first time that she would never be afraid of Mr Thompson. There was something about that face that gave you the same warm feeling of comfort and security as when you put a glove on your hand.

Her father's face was never remotely like that. He worked a lathe in a machine shop and when he got home at night it was as if you could feel the lathe still whirling madly in the living-room. You could feel a wild compressor still driving through his blood: the telly's got to be paid for, the fridge has got to be paid for, it's all got to be paid for – God, let me get out and have a drink somewhere.

'You've only just got home,' she said to him once. 'You don't have to go out again yet, do you?'

'Stop jawing. I'll mark you if you don't stop jawing. You got the telly to sit with, ain't you? Sit and watch the telly. I slave enough to get the telly, don't I?'

'Go and get yourself an ice-cream,' her mother said. 'Put that in your mouth. I'm tired.'

After that first cup of tea with Mr Thompson she was aware of feeling tired too: not exhaustively tired but rather as if she had been sitting for a long time in a too-warm room. The strong fresh air in the woods seemed to drug her and presently her eyes started to drift drowsily to and fro. When she woke she was lying under Mr Thompson's raincoat and Mr Thompson was sitting gazing at the fire.

He was gazing at the fire now, rubbing his two-day-old beard with thumb and forefinger. He reckoned it was time to git himself a shave, she heard him say.

This pleased her; the grave brown eyes started lighting up.

She would be able to hold up the mirror for Mr Thompson. It was only a cracked pocket mirror with some of the quick-silver worn off the back, but it pleased her to hold it for Mr Thompson.

'Had enough tea?' he said. 'I'll have to take the kettle down to the brook and fill it if I'm going to git a shave.'

'I could drink another cup.'

He poured the rest of the tea out for her and she said:

'There was something I was going to ask you.'

'Yes?'

'Don't you ever go back home nowhere?'

'Puzzle me to,' Mr Thompson said. 'I –'

'You mean you haven't got a house?'

'Had one once,' he said. 'A doodle-bug fell on it. My mother was in it. There was just a big pile of rubble when I got home.'

'What did you do after that?'

'Started walking.'

'Walking where?'

'Up and down the country.'

'Nowhere particular?'

'Nowhere particular.'

Sipping her tea, she asked him then if he never worked and Mr Thompson said no, he never did. His mother had had a bit of money tucked away in the bank. It was his now and it did him for most things.

'Fancy never working,' she said. The images of her parents danced frantically on the stage of her mind, like grotesque and desperate puppets on a treadmill.

'As long as nobody don't make me,' Mr Thompson said, 'I don't see no reason to.'

He laughed. He didn't often laugh and when he did so it was with a dry sort of cough, partly a chuckle. No, he didn't work and, funny thing, he didn't read no newspapers either. So that was another thing that never bothered him much: all that business about what was going on.

'I don't bother people either,' he said, 'and most of the time people don't bother me.'

'Was that why you let me come along with you?'

'People quite often come along with me,' Mr Thompson said.

'Walk a mile or two with me and then go back. Company, I suppose.'

'You like company? You ever get lonely?'

'I like company sometimes.'

'I don't think I'd ever be lonely with you. I like it with you.'

'Perhaps you would, after a time. You can very often be lonelier with people than without them, I say.'

Throughout this conversation she was again aware of feeling a growing sense of security and comfort about her, like the drawing on of a glove, and she was almost disappointed when Mr Thompson at last got to his feet, picked up the kettle again and said he was off to the brook to fetch water.

'I'll pack things up a bit,' she said. 'I'll wash up when you get back. Will you bring some water-cress?'

'Might do,' Mr Thompson said, 'if I see any.'

Mr Thompson struck off through the undergrowth of hazels. In a few open spaces thick bracken, turning fox brown already, grew higher than a man. A jay, like blue fire, flew suddenly over one of these spaces with a throaty screech, filling the wood with echoes that seemed to go zithering away far into the deep mass of branches.

Something about these noises disturbed Mr Thompson; he stopped and stared about him. The presence of the girl had never really worried him very much; he had never laid a finger on her; she was just another companion on the way. She'd turn back all right when she wanted to – she'd get homesick or bored, or something else would make her go.

He waited, listening, but within half a minute the wood was deadly quiet again. The girl was right: there was hardly a bird to make a sound. She'd been quick, he thought, to sense the absence of the birds. There was a funny feeling about a wood when the birds weren't there.

The big wood ended in a line of yews and white-beam, at the bottom of a slope. A brook, six or eight feet wide, ran round its boundaries in a deep curve. There were a few deep pools in it and the night before last Mr Thompson had had four fair-sized perch out of it and he and the girl had had them fried for supper. She had never tasted anything in all her life like that, she said.

He remembered how she had sat sucking the perch bones as if every single one was a precious needle of sugar. That was the best fish she ever tasted, she said. You didn't get fish like that out of a fried fish shop. Up to then that was the only kind she'd ever had.

Stooping to fill the kettle from the brook Mr Thompson was aware of a sudden uneasiness again. Thin white saucers of mist were forming and floating across the meadows beyond the wood and out of them Mr Thompson could suddenly have sworn he heard another cry, followed by another, from a jay.

He was walking back up the slope before it came to him that what he had heard was the whining of a dog. He went back a few yards and stared across the meadows, listening. The sound of whining, this time of more than one dog, reached him again. It was quite a long way off yet and it had that eerie sound that hounds make when they're hungry.

Uneasy for the first time, he walked back through the wood to the girl. He found she had been busy collecting bracken and laying a pile of it out for herself as part of a fresh bed. She had made up the fire too and it was ready for the kettle.

He put the kettle on to boil. She was pleased to see him back, she said. She could wash up now and help him when he shaved.

Mr Thompson rubbed his beard with the ball of his thumb and didn't say anything.

'You know what you said you might get down at the brook,' she said. 'Remember? Water-cress.'

Yes, Mr Thompson remembered the water-cress. Didn't see any, though, he said.

'Perhaps we'll get some tomorrow.'

It was half in Mr Thompson's mind to say that there wouldn't be any tomorrow, but he said nothing and merely pushed the kettle farther into the fire. He didn't like the water too hot for shaving and a few moments later he washed out the coffee tin, filled it with warm water and then started to lather his face.

'Give me the mirror and I'll hold it for you,' she said. 'I like doing that.'

He seemed, she thought, to take an extra long time to lather his face. While she waited for him she took off her shoes and sat gravely watching him. He seemed preoccupied and thoughtful and now and then he lifted his head sharply, listening. While he was slowly lathering himself she washed up the cup, billycan, knife and plate. The lingering taste of mushrooms still clung to her mouth and now and then she licked her lips slowly with her tongue.

It was about six o'clock when Mr Thompson began to shave. She squatted in front of him, brown eyes grave again, and held the mirror so that he could see. It would be dark in less than an hour from now and when it was dark Mr Thompson would make up the fire. It was the moment of the day she longed most deeply for. She didn't dread the darkness – not like she did at home. It was all so silent and shut away. That dead smell of the house wasn't there and the big circle of outer darkness framed the central core of crimson firelight, across which Mr Thompson would presently gaze at her and say 'You'd better git your sleep now.' The birds, except perhaps for the last croak of a roosting pheasant, would all be silent by that time and presently she would lie down on one side of the fire and go to sleep, with Mr Thompson dozing on the other.

In the morning the autumn singing of the birds would wake her and she would experience once again the extraordinary sense of not belonging to anyone or anywhere, as Mr Thompson did, and of being free.

Suddenly Mr Thompson gave a sharp impatient exclamation. She saw that he had nicked the upper part of one cheek with his safety-razor, drawing blood. In a sharp turn of his head, as if attracted again by a sudden far-off sound, he had forgotten to take the razor away. The half-shaven face, white here and there with lather, stained for an inch or two with blood, looked grotesquely ill-at-ease. She hadn't seen it look like that before.

'I'm sorry,' she said. 'I didn't hold the mirror straight, did I?'

'Wasn't that,' Mr Thompson said.

Mr Thompson, drawing the razor hastily across his face, was sure beyond doubt that he could hear the cry of dogs again.

'What's the matter?' she said.

'Hold the glass straight,' he said and in his voice she detected the first and only sign of sharpness. I don't want to cut myself again.'

The cry of dogs was nearer now; Mr Thompson judged them to be somewhere out in the meadow. He suddenly jumped to his feet and rapidly wiped the remaining lather from his face with a rag of towelling.

'You got to go,' he said.

Too astonished to speak for a moment, she saw him abruptly pour the rest of the kettle of water on the fire. The explosive impact of it tore out of her, painfully, a single amazed word:

'Go?'

'You got to go home,' Mr Thompson said. 'Now. Quick. You got to do what I say.'

'I'm never going back there –'

'You got to go now,' he said. 'Why'd you take your shoes off? Put 'em on. Quick.'

He raised his hand. It was as if her father were threatening yet again to mark her and she was quick to duck. But Mr Thompson's hand was raised simply to perform an extraordinary act – that of pushing his battered hat firmly down, for the first time, on the front of his head. It was exactly as if he wanted to hide underneath it and the shadow of the brim seemed almost to suffocate his face.

'Got your shoes on?'

She was struggling with the laces of her shoes. When they were tied she looked up at Mr Thompson with bruised and frightened eyes.

'What are you sending me away for, Mr Thompson? I never want to go back there –'

'You got to go,' Mr Thompson said. 'Git hold of my hand. I'll take you to the end of the wood and then you git home. Quick.'

'I won't go there.'

'Listen to that,' Mr Thompson said. He was beginning to be half-frightened himself now; he could distinctly hear the dogs hungrily whining somewhere down by the stream. 'You know what that is? Dogs – they're looking for you.'

He started to run with her towards the upper edge of wood.

It took them ten minutes to break clear to the boundary and already it was half dark beyond the trees.

'You go down here until you git to the railway bridge –'

'I'm not going. I'll never find my way –'

'Under the railway bridge,' Mr Thompson said, 'and then after about a mile there's a brick works. After that you turn right and you go straight for the town.'

She stood absolutely still, looking up at his face. She had nothing at all to say. The grave brown eyes were darkened completely, all light beaten out of them.

'You git back where you belong,' Mr Thompson said. 'You be a good girl now. They'll be waiting for you.'

Soon she was running. She was running under the shadow of the railway arch, past the chimney spire of the brick works and into the town. She was running past the lights of grinning windows, into the night, back where she belonged, to where the house was dead.

The Fabulous Mrs V.

IT is now more than thirty-five years since Tom Blackwood and I, travelling home from London on a fine late June evening, by slow train, met the fabulous Mrs V. for the first time.

It was one of those warm pellucid evenings that have a breathless and suspended aura about them and it would have been memorable even if Mrs V. hadn't made it so. The train on that particular Midland line passes time after time over a broad slow river and that evening all the meadows had about them the green tranquillity of some old and eternal pastoral. Even the cows in them looked like classical figures and in the quieter reaches of river the many wide stretches of pure white water-lilies looked strangely uplifted, as if about to take to air.

We were travelling by slow train because, after stopping to see the end of a film, we had missed the express. I continually fret about trains. To me it seems almost immoral to miss one. Tom, however, was the sort of man who, having paid for a thing, found it immoral, in his own way, not to consume it to the last crumb. He was exceedingly obstinate in the politest sort of way.

You saw this in his face. He was a big muscular young man with strong burning brown eyes, a big square jaw and massive cheek-bones that might have been sculptured out of reddish rock. A shock of stiff dark hair gave him a look of almost quarrelsome aggression completely belied by his mouth, which was very sensitive, and his voice, which was slow and soft except when he laughed. Then it started tripping over itself, rather like a puppy having fun with string. And it was that laugh, I think, that endeared him so much to everybody – particularly, as it turned out, to the fabulous Mrs V.

We played a lot of tennis together, Tom and I. His wrists and forearms were the steeliest I have ever seen in a man. He didn't merely hit the ball. He cleaved at it with fury, as with a meat axe. The result was that I was proud if I took off him more than one set in twenty. I simply wasn't in his class. And it was part of the beauty of his nature that he didn't care.

We were in fact talking about tennis when the train pulled slowly into a place called Sturvey, the last station but two before we were home. As the train stopped I caught sight of a woman, fortyish I supposed, in a smart white dress, a small carmine straw hat and a pink veil walking quickly up the platform, peering into carriages as if looking for someone. She walked twice up and down the train and then, at the very last moment, just as the guard's whistle blew, she suddenly wrenched open our carriage door and got in with us.

She sat down on the far side of the carriage, crossed her elegant legs with cool deliberation and let her skirt ride above the exposed knee-cap. Tom and I stopped talking and I felt myself holding my breath. Behind the pink veil her eyes were so blue and brilliant, almost vitriolic, that I couldn't look at her for more than a second or two. Instead I looked back at Tom and I could see that he too was holding his breath.

'Oh! isn't this first class?' she suddenly said. 'This carriage?'

Tom said he was afraid it wasn't, and in a high, vexatious voice she said 'How awfully stupid,' rather as if implying either that the carriages themselves were stupid not to have got themselves elevated to her requirements or that Tom and I were somehow responsible.

'You can always change at the next station,' I said. 'It won't be five minutes.'

'Thank you,' she said.

As she said this she didn't look at me. She deliberately looked at Tom. And I thought the look on her face was that of a woman who had suddenly seen something in a shop-window that she desperately wanted.

For a minute or so there was an almost indecent hush on the carriage and then Tom actually let out a difficult sort of sigh and said:

'Well, we'll do that then, shall we? You book the court for three o'clock Saturday afternoon and I'll ring up Daphne and Lois to see if they'll make up the four.'

'What if Lois can't come? She sounded awfully doubtful when I saw her. Should we ask Kay?'

'Oh! Kay's so flabby. She doesn't even try. She's always such a passenger.'

All the time our other passenger sat listening; you could almost hear her breathing into your mind; and then suddenly, while Tom and I were still discussing who might substitute for Lois if Lois couldn't come, she said:

'Do forgive me, but I hear you boys talking about tennis. Do you play a lot?'

We said we did; we were mad on tennis.

'And I'm sure you're awfully good at it too.'

I said Tom was terrific; I just did the best I could.

'I can see he would be.'

Again she looked at Tom in that brilliant covetous fashion of hers but the odd thing was that he didn't seem to notice it. Nor did the significance of those half dozen simple words of hers seem to strike him either.

Then with the most disarming sweetness she smiled and said:

'You'll probably think I'm poking my nose in, but I just wondered if you'd care to make up a party with us some time? I live at Vane Court. We play practically every evening and always on Sundays.'

Sundays? We found ourselves listening hard. It was still something of an adventure, in our stuffy, chapel-ridden little town, to play tennis on Sundays. It was still something to be done in secrecy.

'There's absolutely no formality,' she said. 'We dispense with all that. Just roll up. Don't even bother to telephone.'

We both started to thank her very much when she said:

'My daughter will be absolutely thrilled when I tell her you're coming. We can never get enough young people. And she loathes playing with a lot of old fuddy-duddies.'

Tom laughed, in that typical puppy-string fashion of his, and I could see that it got her. It was impossible for her brilliant blue eyes to light up any further, they were so intensely and vividly transparent already, but I saw the corners of her mouth suddenly twitch.

'We usually start about three o'clock on Sundays,' she said. 'That gives the old fuddy-duddies a chance to nap and the young folk to get in a decent set or two before tea.'

I don't know why, but I got the impression that she didn't include herself with the fuddy-duddies. She was very much with the young.

'If it's good weather we go on playing until about eight,' she said, 'and then we all have supper in the garden. It makes a nice ending for the day.'

Tom, with that enormous frame of his, was constantly ravaged by raving hunger, and he laughed again, I supposed from sheer joy at the thought of food, and again I saw her stir.

'Now you will come, won't you?' she said. 'I mean it. It's an invitation. You won't let me down?'

Oh! we were certainly coming, we said; we meant it too; we wouldn't let her down.

'Promise?'

With an almost paralysing directness she looked straight at Tom. In a confused fashion he repeated the word promise and then laughed again.

'Splendid,' she said. 'Joy will be so excited.'

Joy, I assumed, was the daughter and suddenly, as on an illuminated slide, my mind's eye saw her: blue, brilliant, disarming, vivacious, elegant, a younger edition of the mother. It was all going to be pretty terrific fun, I kept telling myself, a thought that Tom could hardly wait to echo, half a minute after we had reached our destination and she had waved us the friendliest, most vivid of good-byes.

'By God, she's fabulous,' Tom kept saying. 'Absolutely fabulous.'

'Damn fools,' I suddenly said. 'We forgot to ask her name.'

'I got an idea it's Vane. Didn't she say Vane Court? She did. I'm sure that's it. I'll ask my father. He'll know.'

'We'll call her Mrs V.'

'That's it,' he said, laughing again. 'Mrs V. The fabulous Mrs V.'

'There's a daughter too, remember.'

'By God, the fabulous Miss V. too. So there is. I'd almost

forgotten her. Gosh, if the daughter's anything like the mother you're going to have a pretty terrific time.'

'Me? Why me?'

'Oh! I'll make you a present of the daughter,' Tom said and once again laughed, the puppy-string notes seeming to mock his huge frame and tie him in knots of delight. 'I'll settle for the mother. The fabulous Mrs V.'

We both laughed heartily at this; after all, we were young and gay.

The following Sunday afternoon, about half past three, we turned up at Vane Court in Tom's old open Ford, looking and feeling like a pair of half-impudent, vainglorious cockatoos.

Tom had actually bought himself a new blazer for the occasion, a coat of many colours, a fetching affair of daffodil-yellow, crimson, chocolate and purple stripes, with a silk neckerchief of brightest purple to match. I was wearing a blazer too, a thing of white and scarlet stripes, with a silk muffler of red and cream. We were both very brown from much tennis in the sun and Tom, I thought, looked as handsome as a steel-gold god.

The day was hot and Vane Court, which was one of those big ugly Victorian houses with ecclesiastical bay windows built of brick and terra-cotta, had a scorched appearance in the sun. Large lawns, with clumps of rhododendron and here and there a big acacia or two and one gigantic elm, surrounded it. Farther away was a big ornamental pond, almost a lake, and about equidistant between it and the house lay the tennis lawn.

A rather half-hearted mixed doubles was in progress as Tom and I arrived. The air rippled with shouts of laughter and encouraging cries such as 'Played, partner!' The two men – I recognized one as a bank-clerk named Aitcheson, a stumpy little man with a head bald as a melon – were playing the game with a combination of deadly decorum and masculine craftiness. Low cut spinners crept over the net. The differences of sex were being heavily respected. It was what Tom called a giggle.

About seven or eight men and women were sitting in deck chairs in the shade of the big elm and as we walked across the lawns the figure of the fabulous Mrs V., in a very low-necked cream shantung tennis frock, sprang up to meet us.

'I'd given you up. I'd really given you up. I said "those naughty boys –" '

This rapturous greeting actually made Tom blush. He started apologetically to explain that he'd had trouble with his car's petrol pump but she cut him off with gay laughter.

'As long as you're here, that's the thing. As long as you're here. And stupid me. I quite forgot to ask your names the other evening. Ours is Varley. Now tell me yours and I'll introduce you.'

Tom dealt with the formal business of the names and we followed her over to the elm. In her low-necked frock, which exposed a shell-like inch or two of breast, she looked if anything more elegant, more captivating and more brilliant than ever: except for one thing. I noticed that, without her veil, the eyes that had formerly seemed so vivid now looked rather weak. It was exactly the sort of impression you get when an habitual spectacle-wearer takes off his glasses. Suddenly a new person becomes revealed.

Under the tree sat the fuddy-duddies and a pretty dull-looking crowd they were. I recognized a man named Dickson who sang in the local operatic society in a mousy sort of tenor; and another named Smythe, a craggy grey schoolmaster who wore starched butterfly collars even when playing tennis; and two owl-eyed sisters, also school-teachers, a pair of podgy dumplings with the odd name of Spong – rather as if they had originally been Sponge and out of shame had dropped the final letter.

One by one Mrs V. introduced us all. The air was briefly charged with mumbles. It was almost as if Mrs V. had chosen this dull, dispirited crowd on purpose, simply in order that she alone should shine. And then she said:

'And this is Mr Varley.'

A figure wearing a white shirt buttoned at neck and sleeves and cream trousers with a faint black pin-stripe and a green cummerbund creaked to its feet.

'Dee-do.'

Mr Varley had the look of an ageing innocent: a pale crinkled babe who grinned emptily. His hands and pale grey eyes quivered like half-set jelly. It suddenly occurred to me that this emasculated figure must surely be her father when she said:

'My husband is dying to make up a really good men's doubles. Aren't you, Lamby?'

'Me?'

Without another word she left him in mid-air and he stood there as if whipped, sitting bleakly in his trousers.

'And this,' she suddenly said, 'is Joy.'

I stared. Tom stared too. Frantically I wondered by what wicked chance, or mischance, Mrs Varley had named her daughter Joy. I had never in my life seen anything less like Joy than the girl who stood before me.

It wasn't merely that she was plain. It wasn't just that she looked lost and sombre. The straight bobbed brown hair and the turgid brown eyes had nothing to do with it; nor the colourless skin, not unlike the thick inner skin of orange peel; nor the infantile nature of her coffee-coloured tennis frock, with its smocking high at the chest, giving her the air of being utterly flat from neck to toe.

It was something much more elusive. I know now what it was; but as I stood there that hot afternoon, frantically wondering and searching for something to say, I could only feel that somehow, somewhere, something in her had been remorselessly suppressed. The blood of growing up had been tapped.

Long afterwards Tom said to me 'If I'd have had any guts at all I'd have run for my life, but I just stood there.'

I just stood there too, not knowing what to say. All of a sudden I felt inexpressibly foolish, vain, impudent, contemptible. Our cockatoo-ish blazers were suddenly a mockery. This was the girl, blue-eyed, elegant, vitriolic, enchanting, vivacious, of whom Tom in his gay generosity had made me a present. In our moment of disenchantment I didn't know who I hated most, myself or Tom.

Then Mrs Varley said:

'Joy is dying to play with you, too, aren't you, Joy?'

'I suppose I am, really. Yes.'

The voice was joyless too.

'And needless to say I am.' Mrs Varley turned on us both a gaze of brilliant, glassy flattery. 'Of course I'll be no match for you. I see that. How shall we pair?'

I knew what Tom was dreading; I was dreading it too. But the trap was open; we were in it; there wasn't any escaping.

Finally, as we walked on court, about four o'clock, Tom partnered by Mrs Varley, myself by Joy, I didn't hate Tom or myself any longer. I was merely mute of dejection.

In such circumstances my eyesight, normally microscopically good, starts going to pieces. I knew suddenly, during the knock-up, that I wasn't really going to see the ball.

'You serve, Tom,' I said. 'I'll give it to you.'

Normally he would have bantered back at me for that, but he didn't say a word. He just picked up the balls – he always held three of them in his enormous hands – and got ready to serve at me. I knew what was coming. Tom didn't see tennis as a tea-party graced with polite discrimination between the sexes. Girls who played against him knew perfectly well they were going to be cannon-balled. If they didn't like it they could do the other.

The first service went past me like the customary white stunning bullet I knew so well, but if anything steelier and faster. My eyes wobbled; I couldn't touch it. It drew a faint involuntary 'Oh!' from the girl and nothing but the low flicker of a smile from her mother. Under the elm-tree the fuddy-duddies gave a communal gasp at the impact of the explosion and then chattered among themselves, with a sound like that of gnashing teeth.

I could only guess what agonies were grinding through Tom as he crossed over and got ready to serve again. It wasn't really in his nature to compromise; he was too stubborn for that; on the other hand he was too sensitive, as very big powerful men often are, to hurt.

He served. The ball scorched across the court like a fiery snowball. In some miraculous way the girl got her racquet to it and the sheer force of the blow spun it from her hand like a shuttlecock. Without wasting time Tom got ready to serve again, as if he had already decided that murder was the most merciful way with agony. Even as he did so I saw, to my infinite astonishment, that Mrs Varley smiled.

After that I managed to get the next ball back across the net and we had a bit of a rally. In the course of it Mrs Varley was revealed to be remarkably good. She concentrated, sprinted with elegance, retrieved the impossible and had style. I got the impression that she was on stage, enjoying herself. Her beautiful figure had an irrepressible youthfulness about it and she finished off the rally with a sliced smash that beat me completely and that I was moved to praise aloud when suddenly, once again, I saw her smile.

From then on, throughout the remaining half hour of agony, a new hatred started smouldering up in me. Anger also affects my sight and as the game went on I saw less and less of the ball. At the same time I took on a sort of protective role, poaching, playing high drop shots, trying to slow the game down. Once, in a pathetic mid-court mix-up, the girl and I clashed racquets and for a second or two she gave me a stare of piteously innocent apology, eyes cowed with anguish.

'Sorry,' she said and I knew that my crass incompetence had simply doubled her own.

I won't go into the rest of that long hot evening except for a single incident. After we had played more sets, had drinks and a shower we finished up with supper on the terrace. It was a buffet affair and you fetched your food from a long main table and then sat about where you liked, on the terrace steps, on the grass, on chairs.

Some time before supper was ready Mrs Varley disappeared into the house. The girl had disappeared too and Tom and I were left for some time to the desultory mumblings of the fuddy-duddies. At one point Tom and I were actually sitting on the grass when Mr Varley came over to us and, with innocent croakings, warned us of the dangers of this awful practice.

'We're all right, sir,' Tom said. 'We're pretty hardy.'

'Oh! no you're not. It's most dangerous.'

'But there's been no rain for weeks.'

'Even so there's always damp in the earth. You'll both catch cold.'

Reluctantly we got up and Tom said:

'By the way, sir, have you seen anything of Joy? She seems to have disappeared.'

'I fancy I saw her walking down to the lake.'

'Let's take a stroll and find her,' Tom said.

'Good idea,' Mr Varley said. 'It will do you a sight more good than sitting on damp grass.'

We walked across the lawns; the evening was wonderfully embalmed in a soft apricot light. Half way to the lake I started to sense an inner disturbance in Tom. I was still some way from knowing the full measure of his pain about that afternoon but much later he said to me:

'It was like crucifying her there on that court. I tell you it was like a bloody crucifixion.'

'Look,' I said suddenly. 'You go on. You find her.'

I strolled slowly back to the house. A rising sense of guilt about everything, combined with an intense irritation about the fabulous Mrs V. had put me into a mood when I felt I hated everything about the place: the ugly terra-cotta, the parochial-looking lawns, the fuddy-duddies, the baby-faced Mr Varley, the general air of stuffiness.

'Once is enough of this,' I told myself. 'We'll not come here again.'

I walked up the steps and on to the terrace. Among the waiting guests there was no sign of Mrs V., but presently I heard a voice say 'Ah! there she is,' and I turned towards the door of the house to see a vision in fluffy flax-blue and a pink-and-red chinese wrap worked over in a design of flowers and dragons making her entrance on to the terrace stage.

Over-dressed but ravishing, the swing of the arms exaggerated but the face as cool as marble, she advanced among us like a queen for whom we, her lackeys, had been waiting. The falsity of the shallow blue eyes filled me with an infuriated desire to commit some ghastly breach of manners, such as giving a laugh of loud sarcastic candour, but as it was I merely stared impotently.

'I've been scolding the young men for sitting on the grass,' Mr Varley said to her with babyish glee, as if this were his good deed for the day.

'They wouldn't have to sit on the grass if you'd see there were chairs enough,' she said. 'Go and get more chairs.'

Humbly he fled, not merely across the terrace but beyond the outer fringes of my speculation. I could only guess how long ago she had broken him.

'I see you're here,' she said to me, 'but where's Tom?'

I told her. Her face froze. The fact that she too now looked impotent with irritation filled me with my own particular sort of glee.

'They've no right to go off like that when they know it's supper time.'

'Don't worry,' I said. 'They're old enough to look after themselves.'

The look she gave me was so savagely resentful that I might have discovered her naked. To my infinite surprise it made her look maddeningly attractive. The cold eyes were suddenly filled with fire.

A moment later she simply turned her back on me with a shrug of furious frigidity, hitching her wrap higher about her shoulders. As she did so all my nerves tingled. The pink and scarlet dragons mocked me. Across the terrace one of the Varley housemaids dropped a fork and it clattered ringingly on to the stone flags like a challenging sword.

I had never been in the position of hating an attractive woman before and it coloured all my thoughts and emotions as, two hours later, Tom and I drove home in the summer darkness.

'I'll be damned if I ever go there again,' I said. 'What a crowd. That bumbling snob Aitcheson. That self-opinionated beetle – the dark chap, stockbroker, what's his name? And the women – by God, the women, Tom, the women.'

Tom remained thoughtful. When he spoke at last it was with a level and quite unintentional air of reproach that maddened me afresh.

'You do what you like, of course,' he said. 'But I shall be going again. As often as they'll have me.'

For the remaining two months of that summer we went over to Vane Court two or three or sometimes even four evenings a week and always on Sundays. For the most part we went

together, but just occasionally Tom was there alone. I myself
went alone just once, but that was much later.

Tom's atonement for that first Sunday crucifixion took the
form of deepening gentleness. He was normally a buoyant,
laughing man, exuberant of health, quick-witted, full of bound-
less athletic charm. Girls, very naturally, adored him and between us we knew some beautiful ones.

But now he turned to Joy. At first I thought it merely a matter
of pity. He was sorry for her; I was sorry for her myself. Then
I began to notice little things, infinitesimal gestures and intona-
tions, small covert acts, that put it in a different light for me.

The strange thing was – or perhaps it wasn't very strange –
that the fabulous Mrs V. didn't appear to notice these things. It
was exactly as if she was emotionally colour-blind. To me, as the
summer went on, Joy Varley appeared like a long-darkened
window with a sudden light in it. It was equally impossible to
miss the flowering of devotion in Tom as he brought cups of tea
to her, moved chairs, fetched wraps, carried racquets and gradually, with great patience, even taught her to play tennis well.

The very nature of all this was quite unobtrusive. Young love
so often erupts with violent physical enthusiasm that it perhaps
wasn't so very surprising that Mrs Varley mistook it all for a
purely platonic sort of all-play-games-together affair. It was
pure all right; but the fires were burning darkly.

Nevertheless it still astonishes me that she didn't notice other
things, subtle though they were. Exactly as she had broken
Lamby – I once called him Baby Lamb, but Tom took it coldly –
so she had sucessfully barred Joy behind the door of childhood.
The girl of nearly twenty-four had looked, on that first
Sunday afternoon, in the agony of her crucifixion, not much
more than sixteen: infinitely gauche, clumsy as a fledgling
pushed from a nest, piteously unawoken.

Now she began to grow up. The neck line of her dresses
gradually lowered a little; the hems of her dresses rose. The
flatness went out of her. While you still couldn't call her radiant
she sometimes brought cries of astonishment from onlookers
when she suddenly rose, gazelle-like, for a smash across the nets
or did a swift double roll, laughing, if she fell. But these spirited

and agile manifestations of love were not, it seemed, for Mrs V.

In point of fact I had something to do with that curious blindness of hers myself. As the weeks of the summer went by and August eventually showered thunder-rain on the surrounding fields of corn I found that the fabulous Mrs V. angered and attracted me so much that my only defence was to flirt with her.

To have been serious with her could only have been hell; to flirt with her gave sparkle to summer evenings, especially after darkness fell, and she seemed to like it very much.

One evening, after tennis was over, the two of us were sitting in deck chairs at the foot of the terrace; the day had finally faded; the air was still warm but full of the threat of rain and somewhere at the back of the house Tom and Joy were stowing away the tennis net.

Suddenly a light went on in an upstairs window – it might have been Baby Lamb going up to bed – and a long golden shaft fell brightly down to the lawns. For a few seconds before the light went out again the fabulous Mrs V. sat so fabulously illuminated, all elegantly gold, that as soon as it was dark again I suddenly reached over and kissed her lightly behind the ear, one hand at the same time on her left breast.

'I don't know what you intended by that but it was very, very naughty.'

'Pretend you don't like it.'

'It isn't whether I like it or not. It just isn't done.'

'It is done. I've done it.'

'Do you know where your hand is?'

'I should know. I put it there.'

'Take it away.'

'If you insist. Do you insist?'

She showed no sign of insisting but said instead:

'Do you go round taking liberties of this sort with all married women?'

'Only the most beautiful ones.'

'You're very young to have experience of this sort of thing.'

'That's where you're wrong. It's experience I'm trying to gain.'

'You flatter yourself if you think you're going to gain it here.'

'I've gained it already. I learn very quickly.'

Suddenly for some reason I remembered how much I had hated her that first Sunday. A sudden combined fire of dislike and attraction went bounding through me and I suddenly ran my hand full across her breasts and kissed her full on the mouth. Everything about her at that moment might have belonged to a young girl. Her lips were unresistant and softly moist. She breathed excitely and her breasts were taut and unrelaxed in my hands.

'I don't think you'd better come here any more,' she said at last, 'if this sort of thing is to go on.'

'You like it. Isn't it what you wanted?'

'I didn't say I liked it –'

'You look so young,' I said, 'so marvellously young.'

After I had kissed her again she said:

'Did experience teach you to say that or merely instinct?'

'My eyes,' I said. 'I don't need more than my eyes.'

A moment later I was quick to hear footsteps on the terrace and I broke away.

'Why this sudden rush of discretion?'

'I think I hear Tom and Joy coming back.'

She laughed.

'Thank Heaven it's not you she's with,' she said. 'At least she's safe with Tom.'

Heavy August rain began to spoil the summer. The lawns grew lush and acid green. Corn lay beaten to matting in the fields and we played less and less tennis as the month drew on.

I was surprised therefore on a thundery but rainless evening to hear Tom's car draw up outside our house and to hear Tom say as I went out to him:

'I'm going over to Vane Court. I thought you'd like to come along.'

'But there'll be no tennis, surely.'

'I know. Hop in all the same. I want to talk to you.'

As I got into the car I noticed a pig-skin suitcase lying on the back seat of the car with Tom's mackintosh thrown down beside it.

'What's the idea of the suitcase?'

I suppose we drove for fully a quarter of a mile before Tom answered the question.

'I'm going away.'

'Sudden. You might tell a bloke.'

'We didn't arrange it till last night.'

'We?'

Again he drove for a considerable distance before answering.

'I'm going away with Joy,' he said at last. 'We're going to be married tomorrow.'

'Good God.'

It was now my turn to have nothing to say but after another quarter of a mile or so I recovered my senses enough to ask:

'Does the fabulous Mrs V. know about all this?'

Tom laughed in a curious tense way in answer to my question and asked me if I thought you'd tell a man if you were going to steal his best silver? I laughed too, at the same time apologizing for being a trifle stupid, and said:

'But where do I come in? What am I supposed to do? Come along and chaperon you?'

'No,' he said. 'You've got to keep the fabulous Mrs V. occupied while I smuggle Joy away somehow. She'll never be able to do it otherwise. I thought you could put on your flirting act for a while. You've been getting plenty of practice lately.'

I struck my knee with the palm of my hand and laughed loudly. This, I said, was rich. Really rich. Doubly rich. With one stroke we could release Joy from that long and awful bondage of hers and at the same time teach the fabulous Mrs V. a lesson she wouldn't forget in a month of Sundays. This, I kept repeating, was magnificent. Absolutely magnificent. This would be the sweet, ultimate revenge for that first crucifixional afternoon.

'Good for you, Tom,' I said. 'I'm damned glad. Good for you! It'll make her terribly happy. Joy, I mean.'

'It all started with that first ghastly afternoon,' he said. 'It wouldn't have happened if it hadn't been for that. I don't know which of us suffered most. It was torture.'

'Good for you, Tom, good for you.'

We drove on and finally Tom stopped the car by a small larch copse about three hundred yards from the house. It wasn't anything like dark yet but the sky was overcast and you could feel the sultry threat of thunder.

'Listen. It's like this,' Tom said. 'There'll only be Joy and Mrs V. there. It seems her father goes off to play billiards every Wednesday night with Colonel Parkinson. Say you walked over. Then say something like "I saw Tom this morning. He's working late tonight. He said you said you'd lend him that book by Conrad and I said I'd walk over and fetch it. I'd got nothing else to do." God, I'm as nervous as hell.'

The elaborate nature of this plot seemed almost childish until Tom said:

'I know it sounds damned involved and all that. But you see she's never even allowed to go and post a letter alone. One of the maids always goes with her.'

We parted a few moments later. He promised several times to write. In turn I said again, several times also, how rich it was and how happy I was and I gripped his hand.

At the house it was exactly as Tom had said it would be. Joy and the fabulous Mrs V. were sitting in the drawing-room: Mrs V. all band-box in a dress of mauve silk with a deep purple belt and a row of heavy amethysts round her neck, Joy more or less in sackcloth by contrast.

As I went into the drawing-room the sun, in one of those fickle bursts so common with August thunder, suddenly came out and lit up the room. The strange brilliance of the light gave everything, especially the two women, a sudden air of unreality that almost made me nervous too.

'Well, well, well,' Mrs V. said. Richly the amethysts flashed in the sun. 'What a surprise. Tom with you?'

With what I hoped was a casual air I spoke my piece. The very act of speaking it and at the same time of looking at Joy made me far tenser than I had expected and I was enormously relieved when she said, exactly as if she too had learned it off by heart:

'Oh! yes, I know the one. *Youth*. The one he particularly wants to read is *Heart of Darkness*. I was telling him last Sunday how much I liked it. I'll run upstairs and get it now.'

She turned with brittle and what seemed to me frightened suddenness and left the room.

Alone with Mrs V. I said:

'What marvellous amethysts. They looked like great big violets when the sun shone on them just now.'

'You're very poetical tonight.'

'That's because I'm in the presence of the right sort of inspiration.'

'I'm very glad you think so.'

I fingered the amethysts, touching her bare soft neck at the same time. I then stooped to kiss her but she drew away with a sort of solemn coquettishness and said:

'I don't think so. I don't want my daughter to come in and find her mother in an awkward situation, thank you.'

'Then let's go where she won't see us.'

'And where do you propose that should be?'

I invited her to look at the evening. It was utterly beautiful now. The dark sky had split completely apart in the west. A great virginal sea of blue lay between smouldering orange dunes of cloud and I said:

'Let's stroll as far as the lake. I'd like to see the sun set across that water.'

'All right. I suppose Joy will be hours with the book anyway. She's always mislaying things.'

'Oh! probably hours and hours.'

All the way to the lake, across the lush acid lawns, I kept thinking over and over again how rich it was. Marvellously rich. So rich in fact did I find it that I was emotionally very excited and as we sat on the steps of the wooden boat-house on the lake edge, staring at the sky's blue and burning reflections in the still water, I suddenly turned and took her fully in my arms and kissed her for a long time.

'You shouldn't kiss me like that.'

She was trembling and breathing hard and there was a deep flush in her neck.

'You're a very beautiful woman. You know that.'

'A little flirting is one thing, but –'

'There's something about the evening too,' I said. 'You can

feel a sort of pulse in it. Beating all the time. Can't you feel it?'

'Don't. You make me think things I shouldn't –'

'Don't think. Just feel. Feel it in the air.'

I kept her there for nearly an hour, kissing and fondling her, exciting her and giving her in full measure the kind of flattery she always wanted. The sun went down across the little lake with sulphurous and splendid fire. Even the stalks of the distant reeds were backed with wonderful sparks of light. In the heart of one shadowy embrace a fish jumped from the water with the loud noise of a pulled cork and presently she broke from me and said:

'We *must* go back. We absolutely *must*. Joy will wonder what on earth – Goodness, my hair. And you've pulled two buttons off my dress. Goodness what *have* you done to me?'

'I hope I've paid you back for all the pleasure you've given me.'

We walked slowly back across the already dewy lawns in the smouldering half-light. It's really very rich, Tom, my mind kept saying. Really damn rich. It's been a pleasure to have been of service, old boy.

When we finally reached the house there were lights in the hall but the drawing-room was still in darkness. We went in and the fabulous Mrs V. switched on the lights and said:

'That's strange. I thought Joy would still be here. It's very rude of her if she's gone to bed.'

'She's probably really mislaid that book.'

'I'll look in her room when I go upstairs. I've got to repair some of the damage you've inflicted. You're incorrigible. You're very naughty –'

'Good,' I said.

I suppose it must have been fully a quarter of an hour before I heard her voice in the hall outside, talking to one of the maids, and the maid's voice saying in reply:

'No, ma'am, I haven't seen her. I've been in my room for the last hour, turning up the hem of a dress.'

'It's very odd. She can't have gone out. She never goes out in the evenings.'

A few moments later she came into the drawing-room. She

had tidied her hair and thrown a light chiffon scarf of petunia pink round her neck so that it discreetly covered the gaps made by the missing buttons.

'It's very strange,' she said. 'Joy's nowhere to be seen. She just seems to have vanished. It isn't like her –'

'Probably gone out to post a letter.'

'Oh! she never goes to the post alone.'

I longed to delay and savour the ultimate moment a little longer. It was a moment of great relish to me.

'She's probably run away,' I said.

'Oh! don't be preposterous.'

'It has been known to happen to girls.'

She looked at me quickly, mouth hard. The look wasn't quite one of suspicion. It was rather restlessly intuitive; and for a moment it threw me off my guard.

'What made you say that?'

'Oh! nothing.'

She looked at me again. This time the corners of her mouth flickered in a sudden tremble, rather as they had done when we first met her in the train.

'You don't think by any chance she has run away, do you?'

The ultimate moment had come. I seemed to see her once again, laughing at the Sunday crucifixion, and I remembered once again how much I had hated her that day. I remembered too the long weeks of light flirtation. It's very rich, Tom, I found my mind saying again, very rich.

'Oh! no, it's too preposterous. She'd never do a thing like that. She hasn't the – the –'

'There's always the chance that she's run away with Tom.'

'Good Heavens, whatever makes you think that?'

This was the great moment of relish. I spoke deliberately.

'Because,' I said, 'that's exactly what she has done.'

She stood there completely dumb. The vivid shallow eyes merely widened into pained blue gaps.

'That's why I took you to the lake. They're going to be married tomorrow.'

She stood there staring, mute and stricken. She didn't look very fabulous at that moment and there ran through me the dry echoes of an old emotion. Once again I felt I was the vain, impudent, contemptible cockatoo. I had nothing to say either as she stared at me. I had never before seen anyone broken and dead in spirit. Nor had I even remotely suspected that I should one day match her in vanity and I could only stare mutely in return, watching her nurse, in shattered silence, her own private heart of darkness.

I never understood her then and I doubt very much if I shall ever understand her now.

Only time can tell.

A Couple of Fools

'TAKE hats for instance,' Minksie said. 'The mad, stupid things they do with hats.'

Bright yellow fingers of sunlight falling through Venetian blinds lay across the bed where the two girls sat, still in night-dresses, each holding a pale green coffee cup in her hands. From a far distance, through dead calm summer air, floated the rolling sound of Sunday bells.

'Every blessed hat they try to sell you nowadays makes you look all mewed-up and daft and prehistoric,' Minksie said. At twenty-six she was a year older than Connie; she worked as a secretary for a manufacturer of plastic papers who greeted her every morning by slightly ruffling her abundant, fluffy, light golden hair. It was he who had first called her Minksie and it suited her coolly elegant, slightly flamboyant style. 'You'd think they were designed for dinosaurs.'

'Mewed-up?'

'Richard III. I remember it from the film. Haven't the vaguest notion what it means but it fits what hats do to you. Take that thing I bought last week. That purple bucket affair.'

A recollection of the purple bucket, fifteen inches high, in heavy velvet, suddenly made Minksie roll her large friendly grey eyes in mock affliction.

' "It will make you look taller, Modom." Dammit, modom doesn't want to look taller. She's the right height now. Men hate tall women anyway. They hate looking up at you.'

Connie laughed and in a slow, rather lazy contralto voice said the trouble was that hats put a spell on you. They got you mesmerized.

'That's a true word. And if they're not buckets they're flower pots, or waste-paper baskets or something or they look as if they're made out of old sheepdogs –'

'And mangy ones at that.'

Again Minksie rolled her large pellucid grey eyes in mock

irritation, this time rather comically, at the same time running her fingers through the sleep-tangled mass of her abundant light fair hair, so that suddenly she had the look of a restless, playful fox-cub.

'Oh! I'm all of an itch,' she said. 'I feel I'd like to go out in the sun and wear a hat that made me feel like a duchess and do something mad and marvellous.'

Impulsively she swung her feet to the floor and started to pull up the Venetian blinds. In the window-box outside a crowded mass of marigolds lifted faces of purest orange to the hot morning sun. On the lime trees in the street below the flowers of full summer drooped motionless, full of bees, in the heavy July air.

'Do something? Such as what?'

'Oh! something simple and marvellous and exciting. Like bathing in the nude.'

Connie laughed spontaneously and then drained the last of her coffee.

'I thought you were the one who never went out on Sundays? Sloppy day you always call it. Slack-about and sloppy day.'

'Not today.' Minksie ran restlessly ecstatic fingers through her hair again, lifted her breasts to the sun and drank deep breaths of air. 'Bells are funny, aren't they?' For a few moments she listened, fair head to one side. 'There's something about the sound of bells that always seems to call you.'

'Wonderful how you found out. They're supposed to call you to church in case you didn't know.'

'You know what I wish? I wish I was an Edwardian girl, all parasol and flounce and a big high hat with a million flowers on it. And a man with a mind for oysters and pink wine by a river somewhere.'

'Hark at the millionairess.'

Minksie, laughing too now, started to search for underclothes in a chest of drawers.

'Some hopes. All I've got is that. The Thing. The purple bucket.' A hat of velvet that might have been designed for a bishop in a rural pageant went pitching across the bedroom, landing on a dressing table, narrowly missing a vase of yellow roses. 'You could never be gay in a hat like that. It sinks you before you start.'

'You're in a mad mood.'

'Just restless. Just the itch. I feel I'd like a bit of swing-high that's all.' Unfolding a white nylon slip, she suddenly paused and looked with a long glance of envious affection at Connie. 'How do you do it, Connie? You always wake up like a beautiful band-box, just like you went to bed. Never a ruffle. Not like me. I have a fight with sleep all night.'

'If you're getting up I suppose I ought to get up too?'

'And did you know that freckles actually suit you? Your face looks just like a lovely brown bird's egg. New laid at that.'

The two girls began dressing and once Minksie paused, half-naked, again held in a brief spell of bell-listening at the half-open windows, breasts exposed to the sun.

'I tell you what. We'll go to that pub at Aylesbridge. The one on the river. The Fisherman's Arms. I went there once with a man and the publican was telling us how in the old days big shoals of smelts used to come up the river. He said you could tell when they were coming because there was a smell like fresh cucumber in the air.'

'Man? I never heard of this.'

'It was before I knew you. You couldn't eat at The Fisherman's Arms in those days. But you can now. It's rather good, they say.'

Minksie, hooking on her brassière, did a short wriggling dance under her white slip. It fell about her like a butterfly. Her long arms made graceful movements in the air, swaying like ivory antennae, and she said:

'We could have oysters and *vin rosé* and then chicken afterwards and something else to drink.'

'Hark at the millionairess again.'

'I'll pay. I'll make it a treat for you. I feel like that today.' She was sitting on the bed now, rolling on her stockings, one slim leg held straight out, smooth and graceful. 'Of course if we had men they would pay. An Edwardian girl with a gorgeous big hat with a million flowers on it would have a man.'

'If you must have a hat,' Connie said, 'you could have my big blue straw. It's two years old now and looks as if it came out of the ark but if it will keep you quiet –'

'I don't want to be kept quiet. Didn't I have one something like that too? Wasn't it yellow?'

'White, I think –'

'I remember now. I threw it away.'

'You may have done, but I didn't. I'm the squirrel in the family. It's still there at the top of the bathroom cupboard. I saw it only the other day.'

While Connie, dressed now, went away to find the hats Minksie stood by the window, still in her slip, slowly brushing her hair with a tortoise-shell brush that glowed gold-brown in the sun. The sound of bells had ceased. In the noon quietness she could actually hear the level murmur of bees in the nearest lime tree and somehow, she thought, it was like the deep sound of flowing water.

Bees were on the marigolds too, flanks heavy with golden pollen, and one flew suddenly into the room and swiftly out again as Connie came back, carrying the two wide straw hats, one pure white, the other chicory blue with a darker ribbon drawn into a big back bow.

'Slightly soiled, you might say,' Connie said, 'but otherwise not unenchanting.'

Minksie plopped the white straw flat on the top of her head, struck another mocking attitude and bent to look at herself in the dressing table mirror.

'At least you don't look all mewed-up and dinosaurish in it,' she said. 'At least you can't be mistaken for some crabby old out-of-work bishop at the time of Henry the Second.'

'Going to wear it?'

'I might. It needs a bit of swing-high to it, that's all –'

'Ribbon?'

'Oh! not ribbon. Never ribbon. Flowers. It needs flowers on it. Oodles of flowers. Fields and fields of flowers.'

'Connie will run down into the town,' Connie said, 'and knock up a shop that isn't open and buy acres of trimmings so that Minksie can go all Edwardian and have swing-high and oysters. You'd better wear a scarf.'

'I'll be seen dead first.'

Minksie, standing at the window again, with the white straw now slightly sideways on her head, seemed for a moment or two to have become quite suddenly part of the morning's deep embalmment. She was not really listening: not even to the sound of bees. But presently little waves of gayest mischief began to dance across her wide grey eyes, seeming to make them dance under the smooth golden fringe of hair. Her hands began to pluck at each other in quick excitement and she said:

'We've got the marigolds and the yellow roses and the corn-flowers we bought for the kitchen on Friday, haven't we? Anything else? Well, if we haven't we can always pick honeysuckle and dog roses on the way to the river –'

'Oh! Minksie, not real flowers. Don't be a fool. In this heat –'

'Why not? We'll stop and sprinkle them with water occasionally – or something. We'll give them aspirin. They'll revive. Don't be so Sundayish.'

'Minksie, I always knew you were a fool –'

'I'm so glad,' Minksie said. 'You wouldn't know me if I wasn't, would you? Go and get the cornflowers, Connie darling. I'm on the up-swing already. I'll get the marigolds.'

It was Connie, not Minksie, who had the bright idea of wrapping the hats in damped cellophane and carrying them in big paper bags across the meadows to keep them fresh. The blue hat, trimmed in delicate spirals of blue and pink cornflower with here and there a cluster of yellow roses, seemed to heighten the delicacy of Connie's brown bird's-egg face as she stood before the mirror in the bedroom and tried it on. Under a ravishing bed of burning orange, marigold laid upon marigold until hardly an inch of the white hat's brim was visible any longer, Minksie's hair seemed to bleach to a shade of tenderest barley straw, giving her face a rosier, sharper glow.

'We're a couple of fools if ever there were two,' Connie said. 'We'll look fine when they start to fade.'

'By the time you've had oysters and *vin rosé* and something else to drink you'll be past caring whether they fade.'

'I sincerely trust you're right.'

'Oh! Connie, you look delicious. I tell you, darling, you really do.'

'The voice of the flatterer is heard in the land. We're a couple of fools, I tell you,' Connie said. 'We're heading for the drain.'

Grasshoppers in myriads, in almost fiercely sizzling chorus, intensified the heat of high noon as the two girls walked across the meadow path towards the river. Everywhere the tall July grasses, thick and sappy and crowded with moon-daisy and sorrel and red and white clover, were shadeless. The unclouded blue of sky was almost flinty straight above and became softened only in hazy poplared distances, far away.

'Shall we put the hats on now,' Connie said, 'or wait till we get there?'

'I think now. In the shade of that big sycamore.'

Clever idea of Connie's, Minksie said, the paper bags and the cellophane. The freshness of the flowers remained unfaded; not a single petal had drooped at all.

'We'll eat outside,' Minksie said, 'shall we? If I remember rightly they have tables outside, under big chestnut trees.'

Five minutes later the two girls were facing a shady terrace of trees so crowded with diners and drinkers that not a single table remained unoccupied. A slightly harassed waiter waved them inside a bar bursting at the doorway with rubicund shirt-sleeved men holding pint mugs of beer in their hands. Inside it was crowded too. A furnace roar of voices burned in low-ceilinged rooms.

'I told you we were fools,' Connie said. 'We should have known you have to book here on Sundays.'

A second waiter, perky-faced, carrying plates of frosty golden melon, came from the kitchens, gasping like a fish to reach fresh air.

Minksie, tilting her hat to one side, gave him a smile of such destructive charm, expansive as a sunflower, that he actually drew up as sharply as if with brakes, in a sudden skid.

'Yes, madam?'

'Is there no chance of a table? I mean outside.'

The waiter, who seemed to be about to swallow the two hats

in one large fish-like grin, said with his own particular sort of charm:

'If we can't squeeze two hats like that in I'll go to Jericho.' He gave both hats another glance of perkiest admiration, openly and frankly captivated. 'Be with you in two splits –'

'Thank you.'

'Mind sharing, dear? Might have to share.'

'Preferably not, but –'

'Be with you in two shakes,' the waiter said and bore away the melon in a golden swirl.

'Now you see exactly what I mean,' Minksie said. 'A real hat has them in a tiz. The purple bucket would only have put the poor man off. Didn't you hear him call me dear?'

'This way, madam.' Back again, swift as if mechanically propelled, the waiter put on all brakes and actually squeezed Minksie with friendly brevity at the elbow before, with equal swiftness, guiding both girls away. 'Have to share, I'm afraid, dear. For a bit anyway.'

Over by the edge of the river, deep in chestnut shade, two young men were sitting at a table for four, brooding with some evident uneasiness over two pints of shandy.

Wiping up the table and then with swift flourishes the two empty chairs, the waiter gave out a strong impression of conferring great honour on the two drinkers.

'I'm sure you two gentlemen won't mind sharing for a bit, will you? Be a pleasure, won't it, on a nice day like this?'

One of the young men, a dark boy with a hint of moustache, looked shy; the other, older and perhaps shy too or merely reserved, put on a cold expression, rubbing his chin uneasily. It was clear that they did mind sharing; it was not a pleasure. They could only devise unintelligible murmurs to each other and suck at beer and withdraw sombrely into themselves.

'May we have two martinis?' Minksie said. She gave another broad sunflower smile that had the waiter instantly running. 'And we want to eat later.'

'Yes, dear. Yes, madam. Be with you in two shakes.'

Slowly, almost painfully, as in a dream, the two men became astonishingly aware of the hats. The big circles of blue and yellow and orange and pink dazzled and dominated the air like a pair of Catherine wheels. A deep scent from several sprigs of honeysuckle, gathered by Minksie on the way and hastily tucked like a cream-red tail into Connie's large blue bow, fell on the air with light intoxication.

Presently the two men seemed to withdraw, embarrassed, still farther into themselves, retrieved from sheer frigidity only by the warm and perky voice of the waiter, returning with two martinis and the bill of fare.

'Now ladies, what shall it be?'

The waiter set down the two glasses and stood with pencil and order book in hand.

'I know exactly what I'm going to have,' Minksie said. 'I've made up my mind.'

'Yes, madam?'

'Oysters.'

One of the men, the older one, actually let out a short hard laugh, stifling it immediately with his hand and so giving it sharper emphasis.

'Sorry, madam. Oysters not in season. It's July.'

'Hence the laugh.' Minksie tilted her hat pointedly, at the same time raising her glass to Connie. 'Well, here's goodbye to the oysters, darling. They cannot walk with us. What about smoked salmon?'

'It travels badly in the heat, madam. We called it off for the week-end.'

'Goodbye to the smoked salmon.'

'We've got very good trout, madam. Local ones.'

'Trout is for me,' Connie said.

Minksie said trout was for her too and afterwards roast chicken with french beans and fresh green salad.

'And a big fat carafe of *vin rosé*, please. Cold.'

'Yes, madam. Two trout, two chicken, two salad, one fat *rosé*. Be with you in a shake of two fins.'

'No hurry,' Minksie called after him. 'We're here for the day.'

The waiter having disappeared, Minksie stared at the two men with a studious, positively chilling calm. She had not forgotten the oysters; the laugh was still an echo in her ears. With pointed deliberation she took off her hat and laid it on the table with the apparent intention of executing a small repair on a falling marigold. The hat, covering no less than a third of the table, caused the older of the two men to snatch away his shandy glass and stare coldly across the river.

The dark boy merely sat reserved and mesmerized, becoming acutely aware of an incredible feature in the hats. It came to him as a new revelation that the flowers were real. This fact held him for some time in a painful state of wonder while his friend, even cooler now, seemed to find something of extravagant interest in the repeated disappearance of a diving moorhen, a dark acrobat on the far side of the river.

Minksie, putting the hat with a broad gesture back on her head, presently fixed the dark boy with a long, melting stare. Under it he flushed visibly even before she said:

'You won't mind my asking, I know. But when do oysters come into season?'

'I'm really not sure.' He had become increasingly nervous. He scraped at his upper lip, with its shadow of moustache, with a tentative finger. 'September, is it? Isn't it something to do with an "r" in the month?'

'I don't know. That's why I'm asking you.'

'September to April,' the older man said, rather tautly. 'Oh! really?' Under the hat, so luxurious but fresh, her face again had that look of playful fox-cub innocence that succeeded only in making the dark boy flush again. 'That's interesting. Because I remember I was in Paris once and we ate them there in July.'

'Portuguese,' the older man said.

'Is there some difference?'

'Much smaller.'

'Oh? I thought it was larger.'

'Smaller.'

There was a certain stiffness in the air.

'Anyway, they're oysters just the same?' Minksie said. 'Connie, we really must remember to ask for Portuguese next time.'

By the end of this conversation the dark boy, teased by innocence of a new magnitude and the incredible glory of the hat, became so uneasy that suddenly Minksie felt strangely sorry for him and was glad to hear once again the chirping voice of the waiter, returning with glasses, cloth and cutlery.

'Will you be taking lunch too, gentlemen?'

'We haven't really made up our minds.'

'You don't mind if I lay the table?'

'Oh! please carry on.'

The two men lifted up their glasses of shandy. The waiter spread the tablecloth and the two men put their glasses down again.

'I hope you won't be put off by us,' Connie suddenly said.

'I rather think we'd better drink up,' the older man said.

'Now that would be just plain silly, Minksie said. She turned on the older man an even steadier, more melting stare, followed by another radiant sunflower smile. 'Now wouldn't it really?'

'I suppose so.'

'I'm sorry we butted in,' Minksie said. She picked up her martini and drained it with sudden relish. 'Won't you have a drink with us? Please.'

'Well, it's extraordinary –'

'Could you stand a martini? I'm going to have another. Connie too.'

'Well, really –' It was now the turn of the older man to dissolve into a ritual of uncertainty. All the time Minksie held him spellbound with a smile. 'What do you say, Phil? It's really up to you –'

'Four martinis it is then?' The waiter, a busy man with neither time nor patience to waste, hopped perkily away, flicking his cloth like a white wing. 'Be with you in a shake.'

The older man, who though not more than twenty-five had hair that receded sharply at the temples, its fairness singularly aloof in some way, started an elaborate and rather stumbling expression of thanks about the martinis, but Minksie cut him short:

'Oh! that's nothing. Forget it. My name's Minksie. This is my friend Connie Alfreston.'

'Minksie?' the older man said. 'Did you say Minksie?'

'Her real name's Elizabeth,' Connie said. 'But Minksie suits her better. It's just her.'

'Why Minksie?'

'Like the fur,' Minksie said. 'I'm the expensive one.'

The man with receding hair looked inexpressibly startled, as if wondering exactly what expensive meant. The realization that the two hats were trimmed with real flowers had startled him greatly too but not nearly so much as the sudden suspicion that Minksie might be well, perhaps –

'I see,' he said, cold again.

'Here come the martinis,' Connie said. 'Lovely.'

The waiter set down the four fresh martinis and, brisk as ever, asked if the two gentlemen had made up their minds about lunch yet? Because things were getting pretty hot and hectic everywhere. He'd soon have to know.

'Well, I suppose –'

'Oh! do,' Minksie said. 'We shan't eat you. Starving though I am.'

'Well, I suppose there's no harm in making a foursome. If you really don't mind.'

'Must be dutch, though,' the dark boy said. 'Must be strictly dutch.'

'What a glorious day,' Minksie said and started laughing in her refreshing playful way so that the marigolds quivered all over the hat. 'I'm beginning to feel all swing-high already.'

Her bursts of laughter started a new mood. A pair of swans, coming slowly down river with five still brownish cygnets, added sudden grace to the scene. The flap of a white wing seemed to break the tension of the hot still air and the man with receding hair said:

'My name is Frobisher. This is Phil Weston.'

The smiles that the girls gave were flowery. The hats almost seemed to dance as they lifted their faces.

'Cheers,' Minksie said and raised her glass to each man in turn.

'I say,' Frobisher said, 'these martinis are good. You don't often get them so good. I suppose you wouldn't join us in another?'

'Grand idea,' Minksie said.

'Don't forget we have to eat pretty soon,' Connie said.

'We mustn't forget either,' Phil Weston said, 'that we really owe you one.'

'Put it on the slate,' Minksie said. 'Charge 'em up.'

Under the influence of a third martini her eyes seemed to enlarge still further. The dark boy grasped for the first time that their pellucid beauty was full of the grey of the sea. Huge and level under the golden flowery brim of the hat they held him in uneasy suspense, so that he was hardly aware of the arrival of trout, brown butter and *vin rosé*.

Cold and delicious, the *vin rosé* woke Frobisher to fresh and unprecedented eloquence:

'I say, this *is* nice. We weren't going to eat really. We had rather a late breakfast and well –'

'Well what?' Minksie said.

'Well, I understand it's a trifle on the expensive side here.'

Minksie laughed gaily again and looked about her at the densely crowded tables.

'An awful lot of people don't seem to mind,' she said, 'me among them.'

'Do you always come here on Sundays?' Frobisher said.

'Oh! no,' Connie said, 'we usually stay in bed and snoozle and read the papers. Or slop about and do jobs.'

'We generally read too,' Frobisher said. 'I say, this trout's delicious. I adore the butter.'

Gazing at the swans, who had revolved on the width of the river some distance up and were now returning, the dark boy remarked that the day reminded him in some curious way of Proust. Perhaps it was the swans. There was some connexion there of course – *Swann's Way*. Did Minksie, he wondered, ever read Proust.

'Generally the *News of the World*,' Minksie said.

Even Frobisher was constrained to laugh quite loudly at this. All his early frigidity melted into air and he almost exploded into sudden pleasantry:

'Look, the swans are coming to be fed.' Phil Weston had noticed it too and was already breaking bread into small pieces in preparation. 'Oh! I don't think so. Much as I like you I fear you're not going to share my delicious bread and butter.'

Arching white swan necks broke the reeds below the terrace.

'Do you suppose they'd eat a piece of trout skin?' the dark boy said.

'You try 'em and see,' Minksie said.

'I don't think one should,' Frobisher said. 'I somehow don't think the management would approve.'

In the soft grey mirror of Minksie's eyes Phil Weston saw the reflected tangle of swan necks twine and untwine like some engrossing piece of crochetry. The sight held him spellbound while he drank *vin rosé* in rapid gulps and thought of Proust again. It was all so like those eternal summers in the France of long ago. What was it? – a frieze of girls? *À la Recherche du Temps Perdu.*

'You're looking awfully hard at me,' Minksie said. 'Something wrong?'

'Oh! I'm sorry,' he said and confessed that he was really thinking of Proust again and how she would fit in.

'Fit in?' Minksie said. 'With what?'

'I suppose it must be the hat, but I think you look awfully like one of those girls he was so fond of describing. You know, sort of all Edwardian and flouncy.'

Even Minksie now looked startled.

'Strange you should say that,' she said. 'That's how I felt I wanted to be today.'

'You're not psychic, by any chance, are you?' Connie said.

Phil Weston said he wasn't aware of it and was once again caught up in the engrossing crochetry of swan-necks reflected in the grey sea of Minksie's eyes.

'I must read this Proust,' Minksie said, 'instead of the *News of the World.*'

'Oh! would you like to?' he said. 'I'd gladly lend you a copy.'

Minksie expressed her thanks at the same time noticing that the *vin rosé* had been reduced to a mere pink centimetre's depth in the bottom of the carafe. Connie noticed it too. By chance the waiter was within hailing distance and in a moment had gone away with an order for more.

The notion of being like a girl in a book had already induced in Minksie a strange sensation of floating unreality and after more wine it was Connie, not Minksie, who started to come to gayer life. Her brown bird's-egg face turned more and more to Frobisher, who now sat rapidly breaking bread into tiny pieces and throwing it to the swans, dreamy-eyed, as if totally unaware of what he was doing.

With still more wine Connie's throat and chest presently became flushed a deeper rose. In the stifling air she kept throwing back the neck of her blue dress an inch or two sometimes leaving the deep division of her breasts startlingly white and bare. Gin, she was fond of telling Minksie, made her amorous and *vin rosé* even more so.

As she turned her beautiful brown eyes more and more on Frobisher she was aware that he too was under a spell, so much so that in the middle of the chicken course white morsels of bread sauce got stuck to his chin and were left there, like blots of lather after a shave, with Frobisher all the time oblivious and not troubling to wipe them away.

Quite soon, while Minksie seemed to drift upwards, dreamy, capturing her long-wanted mood of pure swing-high, Connie started to think of meadows deep with flowering grasses and she lying with Frobisher among them, somewhere far out of sight. Almost as if reading her thoughts Frobisher sprang up, slightly unsteady, and took off his jacket and flung it over the back of his chair.

'By God, it's hot. I've only just realized how awfully hot it is.'

'I wonder you didn't do that before,' Connie said.

'I really didn't like to, you know,' Frobisher said, 'but by God this heat's sort of bewildering.'

He actually started to roll up his shirt sleeves, revealing unexpectedly muscular fore-arms covered with strong gingerish hair. A strange hot leap went through Connie's veins as she saw them and in a momentary daze she heard Minksie urging Phil Weston to take off his jacket too and she said:

'Do you swim, Mr Frobisher?'

'No, he didn't swim, he confessed. Not all that well anyway.

Reduced to disappointed silence by this she thought of Minksie wanting to swim in the nude and found herself suddenly longing to drop her clothes, fall lazily into deep cool water and float away with her breasts to the sun.

'Oh! let's all go swimming,' she said 'What say? Minksie swims like a seal. She's got the figure for it too.'

'Hardly wise, surely?' Frobisher said, 'after this big meal? Delicious though it is.' With something like abandon he threw a piece of burnt chicken skin over his shoulder to the waiting swans. 'I feel replete. Marvellously replete.'

'What's wisdom got to do with an afternoon like this?' Minksie said. She gazed with dreamy disbelief at the carafe, now almost empty for the second time. 'These carafes have holes in the bottom. They must have. We'll get some more.'

'Oh! no, no,' Frobisher started saying. 'You think we should? I'm honestly replete –'

'Replete my foot,' Minksie said. 'With four people at it you hardly get a taste at all.'

'If I can't swim,' Connie said, 'I'd like to lie down somewhere in green, green pastures.'

'Me too,' the dark boy said.

'Oh?' Minksie said, 'really?'

A pink frosty circle waved over the luncheon table, making a repeated bow to the glasses. Beyond it the dark boy could have sworn, for the first time, that he saw four separate flowery hats. For a second or two they floated independently in air. Then they merged again, settling uneasily above the pellucid beauty of Minksie's eyes and the brown bird's egg of Connie's laughing face.

Connie, it seemed, was laughing at nothing, nothing at all; simply for the pure joy of it, he supposed. Frobisher too began laughing, tossing another and yet another piece of chicken skin to the swans. In the middle of it all he was caught once again by the melting beam of Minksie's sunflower smile. He was held completely entranced by the crocheted reflection of swan necks. A reed cracked sharply under the swift turn of a swan's wing and in an incredulous moment he heard Minksie saying:

'Wouldn't you really like to swim? I know a place where we could go.'

Before he could respond to this low-voiced invitation of hers he was aware of the arrival of two waiters. They were clearly twins. Speaking in one voice they said:

'Dessert, ladies and gentlemen? What about dessert?'

'Oh! ice-cream,' Minksie said. 'Lashings of ice-cream.'

'We have very nice iced champagne trifle,' the waiter said. 'Speciality of the house.'

'Sounds delicious,' Connie said.

'Isn't it a bit extravagant?' Frobisher said. 'I'm replete.'

'Light as love,' the waiter said.

'Oh! replete my foot,' Minksie said. 'Let's all have it. It's just the thing for this sort of Sunday.'

The intense frigidity of the champagne trifle presently took a biting grip on Frobisher's bowels. He was aware of it slipping down in freezing streams to his legs. A desire to lean his head on Connie's shoulder was so irresistible that his head actually gave a sideways jerk, as if about to fall off, and Connie laughed uproariously. He laughed too, without point, his spoon shaking so much that a large lump of chilling trifle fell down on to his middle trouser buttons, with an effect so startling that he gasped aloud.

'Oh! the flowers on your hats are fading,' the dark boy said. 'I don't want them to fade.'

'We'll sprinkle them with water when we swim this afternoon,' Minksie said and once again held him in that imprisoning pellucid stare.

It suddenly occurred to the dark boy that they were all talking nonsense.

'Swim? We can't swim. We've got no trunks or anything.'

'In this place I told you about,' Minksie said, 'you don't need any.'

Frobisher, rising with groping astonishment from trying to spoon trifle from his trouser buttons, expressed the alarmed opinion that they must all be mad. On Sunday too.

'They're fading,' Phil Weston said. 'The roses are going first.'

'Are they?' Frobisher said, 'are they? Where? Let's see,' and tried gropingly but unsuccessfully to get up. A certain glassiness sat on his eyes. He licked his lips uncertainly several times and asked at last what time it was. 'Ought to be trotting along, don't you think? Pretty soon?'

'Fading, all fading,' Phil Weston said.

'Oh! coffee first,' Minksie said.

'That's it,' Frobisher said, 'lashings and lashings of coffee. Best idea yet.'

'You were talking about Proust,' Minksie said. 'When can I have the book?'

It was a real lovely swing-high of a day, she thought. She felt absolutely great. First the hats and then she like a girl in a book and then the *vin rosé* and the champagne trifle and the thought of swimming in the nude

'Was I? Proust?'

'All those girls, you said.'

'Lots of girls in Proust,' he confided deeply. 'Always lots of girls.'

'I'll bet you're great with them too.'

'Me?' The flowers were fading rapidly and it made it all the worse because there were so many of them to fade. Acres and acres of them. All fading. 'Me?'

This monosyllabic pronouncement was all his lips could manage. By contrast the tones of Connie's voice were distinct and clear and untroubled as she said:

'The swans have gone. It's no use trying to feed them now.'

Frobisher, pausing in the act of whisking a spoonful of trifle riverwards, murmured in a stuttering, directionless sort of way that he'd be damned. She didn't mean it? They'd been there a moment ago.

'Well, they've gone now. Wise things. For a nice cool swim.' The champagne trifle had stimulated once again the more amorous of her thoughts. She actually laid a hand on Frobisher's shoulder, whispering, 'Got a car?'

'We walked. Morning was so delicious.'

'You're a pet anyway,' she said and kissed him lightly on the ear.

It was half past three before the coffee came. By now most

of the tables were empty but whenever the dark boy could focus them they seemed to be populated afresh. Strange figures wandered between them and one of these, he suddenly realized, was Frobisher. With flailing arms he was navigating a spiral course towards the pub.

'I ought to pay a visit too,' the dark boy tried to say and sat in remote surprise at the inarticulate nature of the sentence that emerged. It had nothing whatever to do with what he wanted to say. 'All faded yet? Yes? Didn't want them to fade.'

'One thing I'd adore,' Minksie said, 'would be a nice cold Kirsch.'

But presently when the waiter came again it was to say, first, that the bar was closed for the afternoon and then, in the perkiest and most natural of voices, that he'd taken the liberty of ordering a taxi.

'Taxi?' Minksie said. 'What taxi?'

'What on earth for?' Connie said.

'For the gentleman,' the waiter said, 'what just fell down. He went a terrible bang.'

No swim, Connie thought, no meadows.

The dark boy, with a tremendous, earnest lurch, staggered to his feet.

'Poor old Frobisher –'

'I've got you, sir,' the waiter said, catching the drooping dark boy, and at the same time with the calmest of glances at Minksie laid the bill on the table. 'May I leave it with you, dear? I don't think the two gents –'

Minksie took off her fading crown of marigolds and laid it on the table. Connie took off her hat too. The dark boy was borne like a lurching dummy into the distance. A brief chorus of small sharp croaks showed that the swans were back again and in a moment their entangled white necks were dancing in Minksie's eyes.

'How much are we sunk for?' Connie said.

Minksie lowered her swan-filled eyes, laughing loudly, and looked at the bill.

'It'll break us for the week. Both of us.'

'I told you we were a couple of fools.'

Minksie picked up her golden hat, stared with dancing eyes at the fading flowers and laughed again.

'Lovely to be a fool,' she said. 'Marvellous. Just to be all swing-high and a fool. The others miss so much.'

A moment later she threw her hat of fading flowers into the water. Connie threw hers in too and presently the swans were pecking inquisitively at the crowns of marigold and honeysuckle and cornflower and rose as they floated away.

'See what a good hat can do,' Minksie said. 'Well, better see if they'll take a cheque.'

The Ginger-Lily Girl

I HARDLY know why I always thought of her as the ginger-lily girl, except that it might have been because the flowers and flower-buds of the ginger-lily make big strenuous plaits in their thick stems exactly like the long coarse plaits of her hair.

Her feet were enormous, with the polished dark underskin and massive breadth that comes of never wearing shoes. Her legs were of even thickness all the way up, shining and equally massive, like stilts of golden mahogany. Her *pareu*, like those of all other Tahitian girls, was red and white, with a brilliant fresh design of pineapples repeated all over it, but in her case it seemed to cover the body of a mare. Her hands seemed even larger than her feet: great golden-brown scoops which she seemed to use mostly for plaiting and tugging at the two vast blue-black coils of her hair, which in turn reached well below the huge round hips and thighs. The top of the *pareu* wound itself across her body beneath the arm-pits, making it really seem as if she carried two enormous solid pineapples underneath it, leaving the broad golden shoulders naked.

The face that went with all this had dull smoky brown eyes that had the slightest cast in them. The nose was flattened. It squared off, more like a snout, with two wide deep nostrils that looked like the tops of a twin-necked bottle without its corks. The brow was so low that her hair, parted in the middle and swept away, gave it a depressed and triangular look, the base of the triangle being the single charcoal line of her brows.

At some time or other the mouth, with its thick lips heavily curled and pouching, appeared to have received a blow from something swung with great force: the spar of a fishing-boat perhaps, but more likely the shell of a coconut or a stick of sugar cane. The wound, badly stitched or probably not even stitched at all, had healed in a scar that stretched half way to the cheek, looking like the red lace-holes of a shoe. She might just as well, in fact, have been born with a hare-lip, except that even that would have been kinder and less fearsome than a scar that gave her face the appearance of being perpetually stiffened in a sneer.

Every morning, when she brought us breakfast on the terrace facing the long lagoon, across which the mountains of the island of Moorea rose like brown-green chimney stacks, she always wore a flower in her hair: generally a large single hibiscus of pure yellow fixed flat to the side of her head, so that the long central stamen stuck out like a snake tongue.

Even the fresh wide flower did nothing to lessen her ugliness. She was extraordinarily clumsy too. She set down cups and saucers with a crash, as if they were iron pots. She let bread slip from plates to the floor. Morning after morning she forgot the milk, the sugar or the coffee and had to stamp away to the kitchens, rolling her wide cart-horse hips, to fetch them, and even then, sometimes, forgot them altogether.

'Do you notice,' my wife said, 'how she never looks at you? She's always looking out to sea.'

'She reminds me of someone.'

'I can't think who,' my wife said. 'She's so ugly I can't even look at her for more than a second or two together.'

'She reminds me,' I said, 'of the women in Gauguin's *Nevermore*.'

One morning there was something rather different about her. She seemed less clumsy; she seemed almost light and gay. It was only after she had forgotten the coffee twice and then had brought it cold that I realized what it was.

It was the flower in her hair. Instead of the customary big yellow hibiscus she was wearing a cluster of small soft mauve orchids bunched tightly together to give the appearance of a single wheel of flower.

This flower gave her a curious touch of enchantment. With her scar hidden from me I thought she looked quite handsome as she stood for a moment staring out to sea. Between the terrace and the sky-line the great waves beating on reef made a perpetual leaping snow-drift in the sun. Inside the reef the sea was glittering, low and calm.

'Today,' she said, 'the flying-boat comes.'

In Tahiti the coming of the flying-boat, once a fortnight, was like the advent of an eclipse of the sun. Everybody had to go down to see it, just in case it never happened again in their lifetime.

'I think I have a friend on the flying-boat today,' she said.

There was nothing very surprising in her saying this. In Tahiti everybody thinks, or hopes, that there will be a friend in the flying-boat. In consequence the quayside is always a mass of shouting, laughing, waving figures, brilliant with waiting *leis* of flower.

'Did your friend,' I said to her next morning, 'arrive on the flying-boat?'

Once again she stood gazing out to sea.

'Not this time.'

In her hair she was wearing her ordinary yellow hibiscus. Once again she looked coarse and heavy, her eyes depressive under the low dark brows. The slight effect of enchantment given by the little orchid of the previous day had vanished. The boot-lace of her scar was raw.

'Perhaps next time,' I said.

'Yes,' she said, 'he is sure to come next time.'

She stared for a time at the calmer reaches inside the reef, where a few wading fishermen with spears were wandering in shallow water.

'I am going to be married,' she said. On the whole her English was correct, formal and rather good. But sometimes, and it seemed to indicate, I thought, a touch of shyness, she would add a word in French or two. '*Bientôt.*'

'That's very nice,' I said. 'A man from here? From Papeete?'

'No,' she said. 'From New York. I shall be married in New York. *Un pilote.* He flies the plane from San Francisco.'

Before I had time to check myself I said:

'But there's no plane that comes here from San Francisco.'

'*C'est vrai. C'est ça,*' she said. 'But he is changing soon to the flying-boats. He likes the flying-boats. He used to be with them.'

The flying-boat runs from Tahiti to Samoa, and then from Samoa to Aitutaki, with its great lagoon, and then on to Fiji, from which New York is still seven thousand miles away. I did not say anything and once more she stood like a big contemplative beast of burden, staring seaward against the sun.

'Do you like New York?' she said.

'It is a remarkable city.'

'Do you think I shall like it?'

'Most people like it.'

With her big sombre hands she started pulling at the blue-black ropes of her hair, twisting them against her hips. Then she turned to me and smiled. She did not smile so often, I thought, as other Tahitian girls and when she did so the scar across her cheek gave her mouth a touch of stiff and mocking sadness.

'Will you fly back to San Francisco?' she said.

Yes, I said, we should fly back to San Francisco.

'Would you mind if I asked you to do something for me?' she said.

'No,' I said. 'What is it?'

'Perhaps you could take a letter for me as far as Nandi,' she said.

I said I would be glad to take the letter and for a second time she smiled.

'You might even be able to give it to him there. You might even do that,' she said, '*Oui? C'est possible?*'

'It's possible,' I said. 'It's possible we might even fly with him. What is his name?'

'John.'

Far out on the reef a wave hit the coral barrier with explosive thunder and across the inner shallow waters a man raised a spear.

'Yes,' I said, 'but his other name?'

Once again she contemplated the sea, the reef and the distant smouldering peaks with the eyes of a beast of burden, her hands twisting at her hair.

'Everyone calls him John.'

'It would be easier if I knew his other name.'

'It would be easier,' she said. 'But if you ask for John everyone will know. *Vraiment.* Anyone will know.'

When we departed, a fortnight later, there were many *leis* about our necks, as there always are in Tahiti. A too heavy, sick-sweet scent of frangipani, jasmine and tiare filled the air. The quayside was brilliant with garlands of crimson, purple, flame and pure white flower.

At the last moment she arrived with a little *couronne* of soft mauve orchids for my wife, and for myself a *lei* of smallest pink hibiscus blooms.

'Do you still wish me to take the letter?' I said.

'No,' she said. '*Non, merci, Pas maintenant.* I did not finish it. There was so much to say.'

Just before we embarked we threw our flowers into the water. They floated about the lagoon like pretty, empty abandoned birds' nests from which the young have flown. On the quayside there was a great deal of shouting, tears, waving of hands and laughter.

The girl I called the ginger-lily girl waved her hands too. And once she raised her big, golden, ugly hands to her face and blew us, with tender clumsiness, a kiss from her scar.

Afternoon at the Chateau

'ROGER! Roger Baines! Is it? No. Yes it is, by Jove.'

The sudden shout arrested him half way along the harbour wall. The August afternoon was too rough for sailing. A hot scudding wind, almost a gale, was blowing in from the land, setting a whole crowd of moored craft jollying up and down like so many busybody ducks. Along the French coast, for miles, a great span of sand-dunes was smoking, every dune a cauldron of swift white fire.

'First I thought it was you and then I wasn't sure. I waved but you didn't see me. Then I felt an awful damn fool – and then – know how I finally recognized you?'

'Haven't a clue, Maxie, old boy. Maxie – it *can't* be you! –'

'The missing two fingers. There's only one curly-headed flying type I know that's got two fingers missing from the left hand, says I to myself, and I know where they were shot off, says I.'

'Maxie! Marvellous to see you. Terrific. How's the score?'

'Oh! living a life of tolerable ease and comfort, thanks. And you?'

Roger Baines lifted his left hand. The first and fourth fingers, with the stumps of the two missing fingers low between them, made a sort of victory sign.

'Thanks to the two fingers, not bad. Put the old gratuity and the pension together and got into plastics on the ground floor. And what does Maxie do?'

'Awfully little, old boy.' Maxie laughed, mouth and teeth handsome, the chestnut-grey remnants of an Air Force moustache spruce and smart above them. 'It's my new working philosophy.'

'Married?'

Roger Baines, Maxie thought, was getting rather fat. He supposed it was the good living. He was heavy and pink in the jowls. His hair was thinning too.

'My eye,' he said. 'I'm here with Mother. You?'

'Was, but not any more. She told me I was wedded to the business and really I suppose I was. Couldn't deny it. So we called it a day and I got myself a boat instead. But it's damn well too rough for sailing today.'

'You don't mean to tell me you've got it over here?'

'It's the pale green one over there. I was just going to give her the once over.'

Maxie whistled with surprise, saying that plastics were indeed a man's best friend. It clearly wasn't like the old days, when they were with the squadron and life was just a bowl of peanut butter. An inevitable moment of reminiscence followed in which Roger Baines was asked with a touch of dark jocularity if he remembered Auxi le Château? Maxie, with much nostalgia, had been thinking of it only yesterday.

'Auxi le Château?'

'Old boy, you can't have forgotten. You simply can't have. We were on half rations at the time at Abbeville. In that first phoney autumn. It was awfully rough, if you remember. I can still hear a type complaining bitterly in the Mess when champagne went up to three bob a bottle.'

'It's a long time ago. You might as well ask me to remember the Wars of the Roses.'

'Nothing so dim, old boy. And it isn't so long ago. After all we called on her more recently than that.'

'Her?'

'*Madame la Comtesse*. We saw her again in that blissful summer of invasion.'

With a bright burst of nostalgic laughter Roger Baines suddenly remembered too. He actually struck Maxie with comradely ardour on the back. He was with him now. What on earth had caused him to forget that generous creature?

'Too much grindstone, old boy. That's what. Too much plastics. You work too hard – bad thing, work. I think of her all too often. She haunts me. I swim with her in that lake. I eat with her in that *château*. I get considerably worked up, I tell you, when I think of her –'

'There used to be the most wonderful peaches on the garden

wall. And huge melons in great big glasshouses. And butter.
Big blocks of butter.'

Maxie seemed suddenly about to double up with laughter. He
remembered a terrific day, he said, when six or seven of them
were there.

'We were most of us gloriously pickled,' he said. 'But you
were the most gloriously glorious of the lot. Just to impress her
you stood to attention on a third floor window sill and drank a
quart of cider. Remember? You said it was like something in
Tolstoy – War and Peace or something. We held a couple of
potato sacks underneath in case you fell.'

'And did I fall?'

'Two chaps had you firmly by the braces all the time.'

By Jove, they found themselves saying, almost together, those
were the days. It certainly took you back, Roger Baines said and
he seemed to see once again, as through a tender glass, the
large grey château, the colour of an old elephant crouched on a
hillock above a wooded valley where, on a thick-reeded lake,
flocks of wild duck flew.

'It can't be all that far from here,' Maxie said.

'What can't?'

'Auxi. The château.'

In a half dream Roger Baines now found himself remember-
ing not only the château but the Countess. She was rather tall,
he recalled, for a French girl, but that particular feature about
her never appeared to be dominant because she was plump
and generous in the body too. She had altogether an air
of great healthiness. She was fresh-complexioned and fair, in
the Norman fashion, and much given to ringing, brilliant
laughter.

'Did you mean by that,' he said, 'that you thought as officers
and gentlemen we ought to call and leave our cards?'

'It's a thought. Why not?'

'It's a very pleasant thought.'

'Very pleasant. Do you think she'd welcome us?'

'She always did.'

They laughed, again simultaneously, but it was Roger Baines
who said:

'Suppose she didn't? After all, she must be a woman of nearly fifty now. The fires may have got a bit damped down.'

'Can't believe it, old boy. After all, we're all that much older. Are your fires damped down?'

Suddenly Roger Baines felt himself becoming peculiarly excited. It wasn't at all unlike that particular exhilaration he had so often felt in the old days, when about to fly. You didn't know quite what was going to happen to you – disaster or glory – but you knew it was going to be hellishly good while it lasted. It was worth a bang.

'All right,' Maxie said. 'Let's have a bash. We might take a little present too. Say some perfume?'

'Fair enough. We'll go in my car. You can read the map. Unless you can remember the road?'

Maxie laughed again, teeth and mouth more handsome than ever under the pressure of his own excitement, his fingers brushing his moustache with the lightest gesture of self-approval.

'We'll get there by instinct,' he said. 'Like two old dogs following the scent home.'

'I've got an idea this is going to be awful fun,' Maxie said.

After all it was Roger Baines who remembered the road. A bridge over a river, blown up before invasion, had been rebuilt and now shone in startling new white stone, clean as a starched collar across the valley. A vivid memory of the days when the bridge was cut and you had to ferry across on six planks and a couple of petrol drums made him say:

'That's the road. Whipping straight up the hill there. I'm sure there's a church over the other side. What did you say about fun?'

'This jaunt. I think it might be fun. I mean I don't somehow feel she'll have changed.'

'Well, it might be and it might not. Supposing the Count should be there? We never saw the Count, did we?'

'No. The first time he was away in Paris. Wasn't he a deputy or something? The second time the Huns had yanked the poor chap away.'

'Which made it better.'

They laughed again; the car seemed positively to spring across the bridge, and Maxi said:

'When you come to think of it you and I were damn lucky.'

'How? Lucky?'

'First we were in the same squadron. Then we pulled out with Fighter Command before Dunkirk. Then we had a good old cufuffle with the Hun and came through that. Then we got parted up and eventually posted to the same squadron again. Only casualty – those two fingers you lost over Dover.'

'Bloody careless that was, too. Still I always say I'd rather have the pension than the fingers.'

'Yes, you might say it's gone pretty well on the whole.'

It had indeed, Roger Baines thought. Damn well. The fingers had been a bit of a bind at the time of course, but looking back you could say that on the whole the war had been fun. Especially the *château* bit. That had brightened the tedium an awful lot.

Beyond the crest of the hill, where thick woods of oak and hazel and hornbeam were being beaten into deep dancing waves by the summer gale, there was the church he remembered and then, rather sooner than he expected, the *château*, crouching exactly as he recalled it, grey and elephantine, its thick lawns spreading before it between battalions of silver poplars.

'Think there's anybody at home?' Maxie said. 'Looks a bit dead to me.'

'It's the way all French *châteaux* look. I never quite know what it is about them. They always look a bit like memorials to me.'

'Mausoleum-like.'

'Exactly.'

A fairly long gravel drive, beyond rusting iron gates of an over-elaborate spidery pattern, swept round the lower circumference of the hillside and then climbed up through the poplars. Every leaf was whipping wildly in the gale, the sound like that of a great crowd of whistling, hissing people.

'Certainly looks empty.' The jalousies of all the front windows, steely grey in colour, were tightly closed, striking Maxie into sudden depression. 'Still, we can look round I suppose.'

'I seem to remember they used the back of the house more.'

Immediately beyond the poplars the high stone walls of the garden began. It was here that peaches had grown in such luxuriance in far distant summers and where on very hot days you could smell the scent of melons on the air.

'Better leave the car here,' Roger Baines said, 'and walk the rest.'

He was glad, a few moments later, to be on the other side of the wall, out of reach of the hissing wind and the sound of wildly prancing leaves. Something almost like a vacuum shrouded both garden and house in comparatively silent seclusion, uncannily.

Suddenly Maxie said he remembered a courtyard – didn't they used to sit out there on big benches and drink cider in the evenings? – and a few moments later they were standing inside it. Huge smooth flags of stone, across which dust and torn green leaves danced in squirming spirals, paved every yard as far as the big back door of the house, where a huge iron bell-pull hung like a rusty mace.

'Well, we can but ring,' Maxie said. It didn't seem much like the old days, he thought; you could hardly call it gay. 'How's your French?'

'Pretty ropey, old boy. How's yours?'

'I can but have a bash.'

Maxie tugged the bell-pull. The only answering sound to come from it was its own rusty squeak. Maxie, depressed again, inclined his ear to the door, at the same time looking at his watch. It was four o'clock and he said that perhaps *la Comtesse* was resting.

'Ring again.'

Maxie rang the bell again. Then, while waiting and in order to break if only briefly the spell of depression, he raised his eyes to look at the third floor windows. It was there, he reminded Roger Baines, that the incident of the cider had taken place. It made him laugh even now – more especially the bit about the potato sacks. Damn funny.

Roger Baines looked up. He could remember nothing whatever about that incident. He merely felt slightly dizzy.

'I think we're out of luck,' Maxie said.

A moment later he thought he could hear footsteps behind him. He turned simultaneously with Roger Baines and there, across the courtyard, saw a girl coming to meet them.

She was very dark, about eighteen he thought, with large sullen brown eyes, a sallow skin and rather flattish figure. She was wearing a loose black sweater and black jeans and her hair hung loose too. The jeans were not very clean and her naked feet, pushing from under the straps of a pair of once white sandals, looked unwashed and dusty.

'*Bonjour, Mademoiselle,*' Maxie said. '*Madame est là? La Comtesse?*'

'My mother is in Paris,' the girl said in English. 'She will not be back for some days.'

Her voice was full of curious indifference; her lips, naturally colourless and without lipstick, tightened up immediately she had spoken.

'Good Heavens,' Maxie said, 'how on earth did you know we were English?'

Without speaking, she gave him a look that would have been contemptuous if there had been the slightest life in it. Its very deadness withered him even more than contempt would have done and Roger Baines said quickly:

'I ought to explain that we are old friends of your mother's. We knew her during the war.'

'Where?'

'Oh! here. She was most hospitable to us. Most kind.'

'We were Air Force officers,' Maxie said with an enthusiasm that he thought would impress her. It failed completely and he said: 'We were here at the beginning of the war and then towards the end. Of course you weren't here then, so you wouldn't remember.'

She greeted this piece of unusual insight with a stare. It too had no life in it and Maxie looked awkwardly away. The rough hot wind had made him very thirsty but for some reason he was fearful of asking for a drink of water.

'I'm sorry we shan't see your mother,' Roger Baines said. 'Perhaps you will tell her we called?'

'She knew many Air Force officers. Which are you?'

'Oh! I'm sorry. Tell her that Mr Shaw and Mr Baines called.'

There was no hint of promise in the way she stared back. Feeling thirstier every moment, Maxie said:

'You speak excellent English. Like your mother. I suppose you learned it at school?'

'I learned it in England.'

'Ah! you've been to England,' Maxie said, again with enthusiasm. 'You liked it?'

'No.'

Neither Maxie nor Roger Baines found themselves with anything to say. Fully half a minute went by in silence. A pile of leaves, screwed by a burst of wind into a cowering, hissing heap, whisked across the courtyard and died uncannily, without movement or sound, in a corner.

It was time to go, Roger Baines started thinking, but something made him say:

'I suppose you wouldn't mind if we looked at the garden? There used to be such marvellous peaches there, I remember.'

She gave him another spiritless stare and Maxie said:

'Yes, you see we had such splendid times here. It was wonderful. Your mother was so gay.' It seemed for some reason a good time to recount the episode of the third-floor window. He looked up, pointing. 'We had terrific times. One evening Mr Baines stood on the window sill up there – that middle one on the third floor and drank a whole quart of cider.' Maxie burst into spontaneous laughter. 'I have to laugh about it even now.'

Roger Baines laughed too but the girl simply stared.

'We held potato sacks down here,' Maxie said, 'in case he fell. You know, to catch him.'

The glint of a strange smile opened in her face like a bloodless cut and then closed again.

'Potato sacks! I ask you. Potato sacks! It's the potato sacks that make it so funny.'

'Well, it certainly helped to push the war along,' Roger Baines said.

'Of course,' she said and the bitterness of the two words was caustic.

There was no hint of the mother in her at all, Roger Baines thought. She simply wasn't the same flesh and blood. Perhaps she was like the father? he thought, and suddenly said:

'I suppose the Count isn't here either? We should have liked the pleasure of meeting him.'

'The Count is dead. The Germans shot him.'

Maxie licked his dry lips and then impulsively decided that this was the best of all possible moments to beg a glass of water.

'Water?' she said. 'I will bring it to the garden.'

While the girl went into the house Roger Baines followed Maxie across the courtyard and into the garden. Peaches, as before, hung ripe on sunny walls, netted with white muslin against wasps and birds. He then remembered how once, as a special gesture of celebration, the Countess had opened champagne, adding cold peach juice to it and rings of pink-hearted peach flesh, to make the most celestial of all the drinks he had ever tasted. Great stuff. He could taste its ambrosial coldness now.

'Do you suppose *la Comtesse* has married again?' Maxie said.

'Most likely. Anyway the Count couldn't be the girl's father.'

Involuntarily they looked sharply at each other and then as quickly looked away again, Roger Baines staring at the peaches imprisoned in their muslin shrouds.

'By the way, haven't we forgotten something?' Maxie said.

'What?'

'The present we brought for Madame.'

'Ah! the perfume. You've got it, haven't you? The *Mitsouko*. Or did you leave it in the car?'

'We left it in the car.' Maxie said. 'I'll go and get it.'

'I remember she always put it on the back of her legs, just behind the knees. She was the first woman I ever knew who did that. God, it was exciting. Everybody else put it on behind their ears –'

'I'm off. Doesn't bear thinking about.'

Maxie had been gone about three minutes in the direction of the hissing chorus of wind-blown poplars when the girl came back, carrying a green wine bottle of water and two glasses.

Her flat, wholly unresponsive face seemed more lifeless than ever.

She gave him a glass and poured water into it. As he took the glass she noticed the stumps of his two shot-off fingers. Her colourless lips seemed to curl and he said:

'Thank you. It's very kind of you.'

'Kind?'

It might have been a word of contempt. Unaccompanied as it was by any expression at all, but merely by the same extraordinary neutral flatness as before, it sounded like a sneer.

'Your mother was always awfully kind to us.'

'I can imagine so.'

'I remember once,' he said, trying to restore some normality to the conversation by echoing Maxie's enthusiasm, 'when she wanted to celebrate the Liberation. She made us the most marvellous peach-and-champagne cup. Ice cold.'

'Liberation?'

Again the word was like a sneer.

'Yes. You know, 1944, the Liberation.'

'What liberation? Liberation from what?'

'From war,' he said, 'and so on –'

'We're still at war, aren't we? We've never been anything else. Wars have to be helped along. You said so.'

He didn't say anything. He supposed they were still at war. There was an awful lot of war about, if you came to think of it. But not wars you could work up much enthusiasm about, as it were. Not like the old days.

Presently Maxie came back, smiling, rubbing the backs of his fingers across his moustache in that self-approving way of his, bringing with him a large bottle of *Mitsouko*, handsomely wrapped in blue paper and tied with shining ribbon.

'Ah! the water. Thank you very much, *Mademoiselle*. *Merci*. I'm dying for that.'

Eagerly seizing a glass, Maxie drank deep, not merely once but a second and a third time.

The girl watched impassively. Her large inhospitable brown eyes neither changed their expression nor flickered for a second.

'Nectar,' Maxie said. His wind-parched mouth felt eased at

last. 'Absolute nectar. Champagne couldn't have gone down better.'

'Not even the peach-and-champagne cup?' Roger Baines said.

'Not even that.'

'Can't agree. There was never any nectar quite like that.'

Fired once again by the memory of that far-off nectar, Roger Baines stood idly wondering how many times he had, in those two summers, made love to *la Comtesse*. Impossible to remember. At the same time he seemed to recall that one chap, Forster he thought his name was, had rather foolishly put it all down in a diary. For his part he thought it was all a bit much in black and white. There were limits. Better to remember it as a chain of dreams.

'I suppose your mother has married again?' Maxie said.

'No.'

For an embarrassed second or two he felt bound to look at Roger Baines again but he thought better of it and merely glanced at the girl. It was all very awkward. Her face, at the same time, had taken on a curious brooding frown, darkly melancholy. She was silently staring into far distances, as if probing for something: it might have been for the truth about something that had long been withheld from her.

To Maxie it seemed obvious that she was merely sulking. With penetrative insight he told himself that that was her way of attracting extra attention. She had an enormous chip on her shoulder – mere youth, perhaps? Or possibly something else? – he put the thought aside. Anyway, that's how the young were these days – they dressed in black, the girls wore trousers and no lipstick, they didn't wash and didn't comb their hair. It was all a way of attracting greater attention.

So awkward was the silence becoming by this time that he was greatly relieved to hear Roger Baines say:

'I must just walk round the garden before we go. I should just love to smell those melons again.'

He walked away across the gardens, down a long paved path that led, eventually, to an orchard of old apples and pears. There the wind was blowing with scorching roughness. Under every fruit tree a gold and green clutch of fallen fruit lay scattered. He stood for a few moments and stared, picking out from the wind-shaken scene a single particularly pleasant memory. He had made love to *la Comtesse* for the last time on a dark August evening there, under one of the many old, big apple trees. She had been exceptionally free with him on that occasion: perhaps because an enormous apple had suddenly fallen and struck him full in the middle of the back, making her laugh with near hysteria. Love and laughter went very well together, he remembered her saying. They did indeed.

Slowly he walked back, to be met half way along the garden path by Maxie, who said:

'I've been wondering. I feel a bit sorry for the kid, somehow. Shall we give her the *Mitsouko*?'

'I don't see why not.'

'Parting gesture and all that. Might brighten her up a bit. Fair enough?'

'Fair enough.'

They turned and started to walk back to where the girl, still with the empty bottle and the two glasses in her hand, was waiting by the wall of peaches.

'Oh! by the way, I asked her why she disliked England and she said for the same reason she disliked France. What do you make of that?'

'Search me.'

'She's obviously got the most enormous chip on her shoulder.'

'Oh! enormous.'

'Hates war like poison and all that. Probably one of those ban-the-nuclear-stuff fanatics.'

'Shouldn't wonder. I suppose they get over it in time.'

When they got back to the girl she was still staring with that melancholy probing frown into the far distance. She had almost to be woken up to hear Maxie say that he was afraid they would have to go now and would she perhaps accept, as a little parting gift, the *Mitsouko*.

'You know *Mitsouko*, I'm sure. The perfume.'

'I never use perfume.'

The rejection of the perfume was arid, toneless but not quite impersonal. It rejected them too.

v

'Oh! please take it,' Maxie said. 'Do.'

'Yes, do,' Roger Baines said. 'It would give us a lot of pleasure.'

She abruptly switched her stare from the distance to the two men and now her eyes looked not merely sullen and melancholy but old and bruised.

'You brought it for my mother, didn't you?'

Without waiting for an answer she turned sharply and started to walk back to the *château*. She had gone only six or seven yards before she suddenly stopped, turned and stared emptily back at them.

'I'll tell my mother you called,' she said.

She turned again and this time went straight on, the uncombed strands of her rag-tailed hair blowing octopus-like in the wind, until she disappeared.

For a few minutes Maxie stared at the gay ribbon and paper that encased the *Mitsouko* and then said:

'This is obviously where we came in.'

'It is indeed.'

They walked out of the shelter of the big garden wall and back to the car. The hissing lamentations of the whipped poplar leaves seemed louder than ever on the hillside. They got into the car and Maxie laid the *Mitsouko* on the back seat.

'I'll give it to my mother,' he said. 'Unless you want it?'

'Oh! no, you have it.'

'No, you, if you'd like it.'

'No, you. I couldn't care less.'

They drove down the hill and across the valley.

'And what,' Roger Baines said, 'do you suppose we'd done to deserve all that?'

'God knows,' Maxie said. 'Search me.

'Strange kid.'

Maxie pondered, thinking slowly to a bright conclusion, his fingers lightly brushing across his grey-brown moustache.

'We should never have tried to give her the *Mitsouko*,' he said. 'I see that now. The *Mitsouko* was the big mistake. Still, it's an ill wind – my mother will be pleased.'

To Roger Baines the *Mitsouko* didn't seem important. As he

drove on it seemed more pleasant to think of walls of peaches, the smell of melons and an apple falling in the darkness.

'Pity not to have seen *la Comtesse*,' he said. 'Sad not to have seen *la Comtesse*. Very, very sad.'

In the distance a bend of a river sparkled in the sun. Everywhere trees, driven by the summer gale, were in torment. Continuous flocks of dark cloud shadow scurried across the land like scattered helpless sheep.

A Party for the Girls

MISS TOMPKINS, who was seventy-six, bright pink-looking in a bath-salts sort of way and full of an alert but dithering energy, looked out of the drawing-room window for the twentieth time since breakfast and found herself growing increasingly excited. The weather, she thought, really was improving all the time it got better. It was going to be marvellous for the party after all.

The morning had improved so much and so fast, in fact, that all the azaleas, mere stubby fists of rose and apricot and yellow the day before, were now fully expanded in the sun, raising the most delicate open hands to a cloudless summer sky. They were very late this year and perhaps that was why, she thought, they seemed to be so much more beautiful. After all, she told herself, you couldn't hurry nature; everything had its appointed time; everything that was really good was worth waiting for. During all the wet cold weeks of May she had watched the barely colouring buds apparently clenching themselves tighter and tighter and once or twice she had actually prayed for them, in true earnest, against the dreaded threat of frost.

Now they were all in blossom. Great banks of them rose splendidly from the far side of the lawn. As if by a miracle they were all at their best on the appointed day: the day of the party for the girls.

'If that's the telephone I'll answer it,' Miss Tompkins called to the invisible presence of Maude Chalmers, who was very busy filling the last vol-au-vent cases with cold fresh salmon and mayonnaise in the kitchen, 'if it isn't you go.'

No answering word came from Maude Chalmers, her companion-housekeeper, who was working in a silent and practical vacuum at the vols-au-vents, with the kitchen door closed, unable to hear the ringing of the bell that flew with tremulous persistence through the house. Sometimes Miss Tompkins vowed that Maude, who was seventy-eight, actually feigned deafness:

either that, she thought, or her hearing deliberately deteriorated the moment she wanted it to get worse.

'I think it's the telephone after all!' she called and rushed into the hall, picking up the receiver and pouring excited 'Hullos' into it, only to discover after some seconds that the line was dead. 'No, it isn't. I'll go. It's the front door.'

'Oh! it's the smoked sprats! You splendid man!' She took from the fishmonger's man a small parcel, hands clutching it with new excitement. 'How clever of you to have got them in time. They're such lovely things for someone who's never had them before.'

She had read about the sprats in a magazine. They were one of the things by which she hoped to give the party a touch of the unusual, a bit of exciting tone. For the same reason she had decided it should be a morning party. Morning parties were, she thought, different. For one thing they were kinder to the girls, most of whom were no longer quite so young. Some were early-to-bedders; many of them played bridge in the afternoon or had sleeps and later went out to tea. At noon they would, she thought, be fresher, in the mood to peck at something and ready for a well-iced drink or two. They could wander in the garden, gaze at the azaleas, take their plates and glasses with them and chat happily in the sun.

A bell rang stridently in the house again and automatically she picked up the telephone receiver, at the same time calling:

'Maude, the smoked sprats have come. Isn't that heaven?'

'Is that you, Tommy?' a voice said over the phone. Most of her friends called her Tommy; she never paused to wonder if it suited her. 'It's Phoebe here. What was that about sprats? You sound like a warbling thrush.'

'Oh! I am – I did. I feel like that. Did I say sprats? I suppose I did – I didn't want you to know. What is it, Phoebe? Could something be the matter? Don't say you can't come.'

'Not a thing, dear. It was simply – I wondered if you'd mind –'

'Mind? Mind what?'

'I just wondered if I might bring Horace, that's all.'

'Horace? Who's Horace?'

'My brother.' Phoebe Hooper's voice was deep, throaty, oiled and persuasive in tone; over the telephone it greatly belied her years. 'He's eighteen months younger than me.' Phoebe Hooper was a mere seventy. 'Would you mind? He's here staying with me for a week or two.'

'Well, it was really a party for the girls –'

'Yes, I know. But you know how it is. Either I've got to leave the poor man cold lunch on a tray or something or he goes to the pub for a lonely Guinness and a sandwich. He's harmless, really. He just needs pushing around, that's all.'

A sense of uneasiness, touched with disappointment, crept over Miss Tompkins. The fond bright illusion of her female party seemed suddenly to fade. She had created in her mind for so long a picture of the girls wandering through the house, all permed and gay in summer dresses, and about the garden, against the background of azaleas in all their freshest colours, that the thought of a solitary male stranger among them seemed now to obtrude unpleasantly.

'But it's just for the girls, Phoebe. It's all hen, I mean. I'm sure he'll be frightfully, frightfully bored –'

'Oh! not Horace. He'll make himself useful. He'll buttle for you. He'll mix the drinks. He mixes beautiful Moselle cup. I'm sorry I left it so late, Tommy –'

'Late?' Miss Tompkins felt suddenly helpless and at the mercy of time. It always went so much faster when you thought it was earlier than it was. 'Is it late? What time is it now?'

'I make it five to twelve. Is it really all right about Horace?'

'I must fly. Twelve? It was half-past ten five minutes ago. Yes, it's all right about – yes, please – perfectly –'

'You're a lamb, dear.' Phoebe Hooper's voice, smooth as oil, sent yet another tremor through Miss Tompkins, once more despoiling her confidence. 'We'll be over in a few minutes. Heavenly day.'

Breathlessly Miss Tompkins flew to the kitchen, actually un-wrapping smoked sprats as she went and finally saying to Maude Chalmers: 'It's twelve already. That was Phoebe Hooper on the phone. She wants to bring her brother to the party. His name's Horace. I thought we'd put the sprats on the green dish

– you know, the Spode. The green would match so well with the gold.'

'Green dish? Spode? People are going to eat them,' Maude Chalmers said, 'aren't they? Not use them for interior decorating.'

Maude Chalmers, who spoke tartly, was surprisingly solid, almost beefy, for a woman in her late seventies. Her hair was dark and strong, if rather stringy, and untidy bits of smoky whisker grew out of her upper lip and under-chin in irregular tufts, rather as if left there after a hasty shave.

'What about the drinks?' Miss Tompkins said. She was going to serve sherry and gin with tomato juice for those who preferred it, though most of the girls, as she knew, adored gin in some form or another. But looking distractedly round the kitchen she saw neither drinks nor glasses and was unpacified by Maude Chalmers' level, practical voice saying:

'The drinks are where they should be. On the sideboard in the drawing-room. What are people going to eat the sprats with by the way? Their fingers?'

'Oh! forks, forks.'

Ignoring this desperate remark except for a sideways hitch of her hairy chin, Maude Chalmers picked up a large Sheffield plate tray filled with canapés, delicate little sandwiches sprinkled with emerald threads of mustard and cress, cold chipolata sausages, rounds of stuffed hard boiled eggs and slices of toast spread with liver pâté and topped with olives. While Miss Tompkins had been fussing with idle fears over the weather, the sprats and whether the azaleas would open in time or not she had prepared every crumb of food herself. Everything, as far as she was concerned, was done. Everything was ready.

'I feel there's such heaps still to do,' Miss Tompkins said. 'Shouldn't we have a table or two put out on the lawn? Don't you think? –'

In fresh, fussy alarm, she followed Maude Chalmers to the drawing-room, taking out her powder compact as she went. Drinks, glasses, plates, dishes, napkins, olives, radishes, cigarettes and even forks were, to her trembling astonishment, placed about the room in perfect order everywhere. The silvery tray of food brought in by Maude Chalmers merely crowned the waiting pattern.

'Everything looks so cool,' she said. 'Where are you going?'

'To fetch your precious sprats, dear.'

'Oh! I see. Yes, yes, I see.' Miss Tompkins held the mirror of her compact so close to her face that she actually recoiled sharply from the reflection of the one jellied uneasy eye that stared back a her. 'Oh! I look a mess. I'm an absolute sight.' She hastily salted herself with ill-timed generous dabs of her powder puff, making her face look more sharply pink than ever. Powder flew everywhere, prompting her to give three or four spurting little sneezes, cat-fashion, the last of which seemed to be echoed in a gentle buzz at the front door-bell, so polite as to be almost a whisper.

'Was that the bell?' she called. 'Maude, was that you? Did you hear?' Maude, she thought, was feigning deafness again, but a moment later Maude was answering with customary tartness from the kitchen:

'It's the Miss Furnivals, you bet your life. They're always on the dot. Can you go? I've still got to do the sprats –'

Two ladies of undernourished appearance, greyish and wrinkled as a pair of barely wakening chrysalids, almost fell into the house, as if from sheer surprise or weakness, or even both, as Miss Tompkins opened the front door. Wheezes of timid breath escaped from them in matching rhythm, offering greetings that were not really audible as words. Their shrunken little bodies seemed to float across the hall-way, their sharp triangular noses thrusting piercingly ahead, as if already scenting food.

Before Miss Tompkins could dispose of the two drifting bodies with politeness, Maude Chalmers was back from the kitchen carrying in her hands a golden star of sprats, shining on a green dish, phosphorescently. A moment later a car hooted with a challenge of greeting from the driveway outside, but before Miss Tompkins could recover from the start of surprise it gave her the front door was actually opened to admit a throaty solo chorus of laughter, followed by words which came with liquid undulation:

'It's only me, it's only me. My god-fathers, Tommy, you chose a thirsty day.'

'Connie, my angel,' Miss Tompkins said.

She ran forward to press powdery caressive cheeks on the face of a tallish woman in her late seventies who recoiled slightly as if thinking of tossing back the low-cut fringe of her curled coppery hair. As she did so she raised her hand to her hat as if feeling that it might suddenly fall off. Instead the hat, a very small one, sat with surprising firmness on her flaming hair, looking like a white cake decorated with spring-like airiness in a design of narcissi, pink rosebuds and lily-of-the-valley.

'I saw Phoebe Hooper driving up.' Connie Stevens bore widowhood with a sort of metallic serenity, perhaps because a third excursion into it had given her both confidence and practice. 'And with a man. I thought this was just for the old hens today?'

'Her brother. His name's Horace. He had to be left alone –'

'Horace? I've heard of Horace somewhere. Isn't he in tea or something?'

Suddenly the door-bell rang again, to be answered this time with calm and beefy promptitude by Maude. At the sound of voices Miss Tompkins turned with the expectation of seeing Phoebe Hooper and her brother Horace, but to her surprise – it was her day of surprises, she suddenly thought, first the azaleas, then the weather, then – it was Dodie Sanders and her mother.

Dodie Sanders, tall, thin and sallow, with depressed fair hair, had a mouth that was not only unrouged but almost perpetually open in a low droop that gave her a look not at all unlike that of a lean, long fish that had been landed and left on a river bank in a state of gentle expiration. Her eyes were reddish and globular; the lashes were like little gingery red ants nervously dancing up and down.

'Please do go in. Maude will look after you.' Miss Tompkins felt suddenly, as she always did in the presence of Dodie Sanders and her mother, slightly ill-at-ease. Dodie, although sixty, was like a girl who had never grown up. With fish-like coldness she swam away under the big fin of her mother, who in a shining dress of steel-blue silk glided away to the drawing-room like a watchful shark.

'Ah! it's us at last!' Phoebe Hooper, with habitual domination, was already in the hall-way, not having bothered with the formality of the bell. 'You must blame Horace for it. He's such a slow coach. He was simply ages getting ready.'

Horace had very much the appearance of a shy and inattentive prawn: the cushiony splendour of Phoebe Hooper, immense in bust and hips, overwhelmed him. Modest grey curls encircled his crimson ears like tufts of sheep wool and two small sepia bull's eyes stared with wandering apprehension from under mild whiskery grey brows. In one hand he was clutching two long green bottles of wine and in the other a siphon of soda and a third bottle of wine. The strain of this overloading had driven his cream collar and rose-brown bow tie slightly askew and somehow at the same time the trousers of his crumpled fawn suit had become unevenly hitched up, revealing glimpses of white socks that had fallen down.

'This is Horace,' Phoebe Hooper said. 'I made him bring the wine because I knew he'd adore making that cup for you. It's his great speciality –'

'Oh! I don't know about –' Horace smiled shyly. Unable to shake hands or finish his mildly protesting sentence, he stood between the two girls with an air of indecisive, wistful meditation. He seemed to be thinking of something far outside the walls of Miss Tompkins' house: perhaps a quiet glass of Guinness, a walk with a dog, a game of golf somewhere.

'Oh! it's my day of surprises,' Miss Tompkins said. 'First the azaleas, then the sprats and now – this, wine! And of course, the weather – all the time improving as it gets better.'

Horace reacted to these inconsequential statements with a solemnity far greater than mere surprise. The sheer weight of the wine bottles seemed to drag him down.

'You'd better lead him to the kitchen,' Phoebe said. 'Get him to work. Don't let him get lazy.'

'Oh! yes, of course. This way, this way, Mr Hooper,' Miss Tompkins said. 'Maude will find you all you need.'

In the kitchen Maude was topping shining dishes of early strawberries with large blobs of cream. At the sudden appearance of Horace and Miss Tompkins she drew herself straight up, as if about to be tartly affronted, but something about Horace's modest and crumpled appearance made her pause, spoon in air, while blobs of cream slowly dropped to the tablecloth.

'This is Phoebe's brother, Horace. He's going to make us the most delicious cup or something with wine. Is it Hock, did you say, Mr Hooper, or Moselle? I think you need lemons for that, don't you? Do you need lemons?'

Horace, unloading wine bottles and siphon on the kitchen table with evident relief, said yes, he needed lemons and also ice and a little mint, please, if they had it.

'Plenty of mint in the garden,' Maude said, her voice brusque as sandpaper. 'Under the first apple-tree.'

'I must fly back,' Miss Tompkins said. 'I hear the bell again.'

In her light thrush-warbling fashion she flew away, half-singing, 'I'm coming! I'm coming! I'll be there!'

'I suppose you'll need jugs and glasses,' Maude said. 'Anything else?'

'A little sugar.'

'Lump or gran?'

'About a dozen lumps, I'd say. And a cup of brandy.'

'Brandy? All we've got is cooking.'

'That will do nicely.'

Maude, returning from a kitchen cupboard with a meagre quarter bottle of brandy, paused to eye the three bottles of Moselle and their companion siphon with flinty disapproval. What were people coming to suddenly, bringing their own bottles to a party? They'd be bringing their own nuts or something next.

She supposed Mr Hooper needed a corkscrew too, she said. He'd brought plenty of bottles, she must say. Did he want to get them all squiffy or something?

Horace, who had no intention whatever of getting anybody squiffy and who hadn't in the least wanted to make the Moselle cup in the first place but was merely doing so because his sister was a bully and insisted he do a good turn of some kind as a reward for being invited, merely smiled with excruciating shyness again and said:

'It was really my sister's idea. She gets rather carried away.'

Something about the smile and the retreating tone of Horace's apologetic voice made Maude suddenly think of a dog about to cower into a corner after some dire misdeed. She suddenly felt unaccountably sorry for Horace. She knew it was all that Phoebe Hooper's fault, puffing herself up like a majordomo. The woman was always bossing. She woke up every morning, Maude was sure, with great ambitious ideas bouncing about her head like electrons or whatever they were – let's all have a picnic, let's do *Twelfth Night* out of doors or something – and then made somebody else do all the donkey work. The woman was infuriatingly domineering; she made you wild.

Horace, now armed with a corkscrew, pulled the first cork with such clean, snapping precision that Maude was actually startled and gave a giggle and said Mr Hooper sounded very expert. She supposed he was doing things like making Moselle cup all the time?

Horace, who hadn't made Moselle or any other cup since his sister's sixtieth birthday, to celebrate which she had inveigled the two Miss Furnivals into lending their large bushy garden for an Edwardian street pageant accompanied by three cornet and barrel-organ players and a fish-and-chip van, said:

'Well, as a matter of fact, not really. Might I have the ice now? And two jugs please?'

Obediently she rushed to find ice and jugs. Two tall Venetian glasses of rose-purple colour seemed to her the very things for the cup and after putting down the ice-tray on the kitchen table she started polishing them vigorously with a cloth, saying at the same time:

'You said mint. What about mint now? Shall I go and get it? We've got lemon mint too, I think.'

Horace, who was trying hard to remember the exact proportions of the cup's ingredients, put a dozen cubes of ice in a jug and coloured them with a golden film of brandy. Hesitant about something, he stood biting his lip. Oughtn't there to be a dash or two of *curaçao*? Something seemed to tell him so.

'You haven't a spot of *curaçao*, I suppose?'

No, but they had *maraschino*, Maude said, and she thought also a little *cointreau*.

By now Horace was mildly confused. He couldn't remember for the life of him whether it was *curaçao*, *cointreau* or *maraschino* that the cup demanded and again he stood biting his lip with that shy perplexity that affected Maude far more sharply than any look of open appeal.

Was something the matter? she said and Horace assured her that no, it was nothing, merely that he wondered if *maraschino* or –

Before she could allow herself a second of rational thought Maude made the astonishingly impetuous suggestion that they should be devils – they should put them both in!

Maude's unexpected suggestion of devilry was accompanied by another giggle or two, and had the instant effect of making Horace stir ice with an over-vigorous rattling spoon, as if uneasily anxious to drown the odd sounds that Maude was making. Any moment now his sister would be storming the kitchen, imperiously calling for the cup, scolding him again for being a slow-coach.

'Oh! all right, let's put them both in –'

'Do!' Maude said. 'Use them up. It'll be a way of clearing them out. I'll get the mint now.'

By the time Maude came back with a handful of fresh mint from the garden the tall Venetian jugs were looking frosty. A translucent glow of green, fresh and light as that of a half-bleached leaf, streamed softly through the rosy-purple patterns of the glass. Finally crowned by mint and ice and lemon the cup looked, as Maude had suggested it would, very expert.

Shyly Horace resisted flattery. It wasn't after all, the looks – it was, he reminded her, the taste of the thing.

'May I taste?' Maude said. 'Just the weeniest –'

Maude was quick to find glasses and Horace poured out two cold and inviting measures of the cup, at one of which Maude drank deeply enough to leave a bead or two of green on the lower and longer sprouts of her moustaches.

'I've never tasted anything quite like it before,' she said. 'I think it's most unique.'

Under this generous tribute Horace looked shyer than ever. At the same time, he had to admit, the fragrant coldness of the cup seemed good. It had something to it. It wasn't bad at all.

Maude, under the stimulus of a strong second gulp, was about to say again that it was far better than that. The word 'genius' hung on her lips. She giggled again and was on the point of asking Horace to top her up when an intruding voice arrested her:

'What's all this we hear about punch? Or cup or something? Or aren't we allowed into the wine sanctum?'

Connie Stevens' coppery head, arresting as a shining helmet, appeared suddenly in the kitchen doorway. Maude, unable to explain why, felt the moisture all over her body run cold and with a sudden return to customary tartness she said:

'Mr Hooper will bring the wine-cup when it's ready. Things take time.'

Without quite knowing what she was doing she snatched up a pair of kitchen scissors and disappeared into the garden, half-running, beefy hindquarters bumping up and down.

'Everybody's dilating,' Connie Stevens said. 'That's why I came to peep. They all say you're mixing a beaut.'

'Oh! I don't know –'

'The girls are lapping up gin like stink already,' she said. 'Are you trying to get them all spellbound? By the way, my name's Connie Stevens. Phoebe told me about you once. Aren't you in tea?'

Horace, spurting a final squeeze of soda into the wine-cup, said no, he wasn't in tea. He had been in plastics. Now he was retired.

'Nonsense. You look far too young to retire.'

He was afraid it was a fact, Horace said.

'I used to have shares in plastics once. Plastic Research Foundation or something like that it was called. They did marvellously.'

'My company.'

'No wonder. I'm sure you were the wizard.'

Connie Stevens peered with a sort of spry innocence, eye-lashes dancing, into the wine-cup. 'It looks so artistic,' she said. 'I love drinks that look artistic. May one taste? I mean the merest *soupçon*?'

'I rather think it still needs another stir –'

'The artist's touch. I know. Will it knock us all flying?'

Connie Stevens gave Horace a look of slow, exploratory charm. In contrast to Maude, who found herself under the spell of the brown shy eyes, she found herself suddenly engrossed by his ears. They were firm but delicate; they were like a pair of clean rosy fossils. Something about their recurring lines spiral-ling perfectly inward sent the strangest voluptuous spasm through her, so that she felt sharply annoyed when Maude Chalmers burst in through the garden door like a clumsy bear and said acidly:

'Here's the lemon mint. I suppose it goes in whole? Or do you chop it?'

Bear-like still, she threw the stalks of mint on the table and retreated with sweeping haste in the direction of the sitting-room. Connie Stevens merely stared and shrugged her shoul-ders.

'Strange woman. Embittered. I can't think why Tommy keeps on with her.'

Without answering, Horace dropped a sprig or two of lemon mint into the wine-cup, giving it a final stir with a spoon.

'May one taste? You said I might.'

Horace, uneasy at Maude's acid departure, poured out half a glass of wine-cup. Connie Stevens took it, held her little deli-cate hat with her free hand and sipped at the glass with lips that, heavy with lipstick of a deep shade of coppery rose, were designed to match her hair.

After drinking, she paused, held up her eyes in a half-voluptuous glance to heaven and said that some of them would certainly know when they'd had this. This was it: the real McCoy.

'It's pretty mild really,' Horace said. 'It's just refreshing. I think we'd better take it in.'

The sitting-room was electric with female voices and springing laughter. Miss Tompkins greeted the arrival of the wine-cup with rising warbles of delight. Her hands played scales in the air. A whole regiment of hats swivelled sharply to concentrate on Horace, modestly bearing the two jugs, but had scarcely a glance for Connie Stevens, carrying a tray of glasses, until Maude rushed up with something like outrage and took it away.

'On the table here, on the table here,' she commanded. 'Set it down here.'

Horace, dutifully setting down the two jugs on a corner table, looked like a one-man patrol ambushed and far outnumbered. Elderly ladies, gay as dolls, seemed to spring from everywhere. Miss Tompkins warbled, for perhaps the tenth time, that when they each had their cup they must take it outside: it was so sunny, so absolutely perfect, they mustn't miss the azaleas. There mightn't be another day.

'Well, young man,' a clear soprano voice said and Horace, in infinite astonishment, suddenly realised that this could only mean himself. He turned from pouring the first of the wine-cup into glasses to find himself confronted by a neat vision in a white silk suit threaded with narrow charcoal stripes and a little hat, not unlike a silvery pineapple, with an inch or two of light grey veil, that sat slightly tilted on a head of impeccably curled dark grey hair. Lithe and straight as a cane, with eyes as blue as larkspur, she didn't look a day over sixty, Horace thought. 'What's all this about your Moselle-cup I hear?'

'This is Miss La Rue,' Miss Tompkins told him. She longed to tell him too that, as all the girls knew, Miss La Rue was within a month or so of ninety, but Miss La Rue was so engrossed in sprightly appreciation of both Horace and the glass of wine-cup he had by now put into her hands that Miss Tompkins realised sadly that she was very much *de trop* and said only, before moving away: 'You must talk to her. She has the most wonderful memory. Astonishing. She remembers everything.'

'I certainly remember this,' Miss La Rue said. No tremor of age was detectable in voice, air or eye as she lifted her glass and stared at Horace through it, as if with the intention of examining him microscopically. 'I first had this at Ascot in '89. That was a glorious day too. Rather like today.'

She drank, afterwards sucking delicately at her firm moist lips.

'No *curaçao*?'

No, Horace had to confess, no *curaçao*.

'Great pity,' she said. 'It gives that touch.'

She nevertheless gave him a glance of matchless gratitude, eyes glowing with the iridescence of young petals. Receiving it, Horace felt for some reason extraordinarily young, almost boyish; he was suddenly a character in some distant, long-lost school party.

'You're spilling it, you're spilling it!' It was Maude Chalmers now, in rigid reprimand. 'All over the place. Give it to me, do give it to me.' She snatched the jug from his hands. 'You can't trust them, Miss La Rue, can you? You can't trust them.'

In contrast to this dark insinuation Miss La Rue looked, as her eyes smiled under the grey fringe of veil, all trust and light.

'What of these azaleas I hear so much about?' she said. 'Aren't you going to take me to see them?'

'Of course. Whenever you wish.'

Horace, less shy now and suddenly feeling more youthful than ever, prepared to move away.

'Not without your cup, surely?' she said. 'I'll take a little more too before we go.'

Armed with full glasses, they walked slowly into a garden so drenched with sunlight that it gave a fantastic acidity to the brightness of the lawn's new-mown grass. The amazing transparence of blue sky seemed to lift the whole world up. The voices of several ladies chirping about the thick orange and pink and yellow forest of azaleas might have been the cries of birds.

Presently Horace was uneasily astonished to find Miss La Ru taking his arm: not lightly, but in an earnest lock, almost a cuddle. A breath of perfume, so delicate that the mere movement of her arm might have released it, rose in the air. It might have been mignonette, he thought

'I'm walking slowly,' she said, 'only because I don't want to get anywhere,' and looked down for some moments in silence at her feet.

Horace looked at them too. The ankles were surprisingly small, delicate and well-shaped. Each of her grey shoes had a black frontal bow with a single white spot on the wings, giving the effect of a resting butterfly.

'Women chatter so,' she said. 'The nice thing about you is you don't talk too much.'

She sipped wine-cup as she walked along, a feat of such accurate balance and ease, with no hint of haste or awkwardness, that she might have been doing it every day.

'Why was Maude Chalmers so vinegary?' she said.

'I didn't notice it.'

'Of course you noticed it.'

'I suppose the party makes a lot of work,' he said. He recalled the incident of the mint; though so small it now seemed embarrassing. 'I suppose the wine-cup put her out of her stride.'

'She was angry with you.'

'With me? Oh! dear no.'

'Flaming.' She turned and looked him squarely in the eye. It was a look of both intimacy and penetration. 'You'd been flirting with her.'

'Oh! never!'

'Of course you had. She was red all over.'

Ahead, the azaleas flamed. No single petal had yet fallen from the thickly fringed branches. Below them, and to one side, a platoon of delphiniums, palest blue to near black, stood in arrested grandeur, unshaken by wind.

'I see there's a seat over there,' she said. 'It's easier to drink wine sitting down –'

'No, you don't. No, you don't. I'm stealing him. Tommy's desperate.' It was the strident voice of Connie Stevens metallically beating across the lawn. 'The wine-cup's giving out fast. And Phoebe says you have another bottle left.'

Horace, jerked to his feet as by an invisible string, uttered very small disturbed noises.

'Come, come, come,' Connie Stevens said, as if bringing a poodle to heel. 'Oh! he shall come back. I'll send him back.'

'Take my glass, young man.' Miss La Rue drained her glass,

lifted it towards Horace and fixed him with a sort of accusative charm. 'Don't let them keep you. I want to talk to you.'

As if actually ordered to do so, Horace drained his glass too and then, half-dragged by the imperative hand of Connie Stevens, took both empty glasses away.

'Oh! you dear man, we work you to death.' In the drawing-room Miss Tompkins, flushed with gin and after-doses of wine-cup, was full of giddy solicitude. 'Empty glasses too! Empty glasses! No one should empty a glass when they can have it filled up.' She laughed on dithering notes, at the same time grabbing from a table a consolatory glass of something that Horace presently discovered was gin and tonic. He drank at it timidly. 'Oh! drink up, you dear man. You need it. We've got work for you to do. That comes of being so popular.'

Popular? The word, sped on its way by gin and wine-cup, rushed through the chattering wings of female voices like an arrow. A bare feminine arm, belonging to someone he didn't recognize, held him momentarily suspended, just long enough for him to hear:

'Absolutely marvellous, your cup. Making the party.'

Another voice, cooing gently, primed him to beware. 'I'm after you for the recipe. Don't forget, will you? Just scribble it down. I'm after you.'

'I go for this cup,' he heard another one of the girls saying. 'I really do.'

'You can feel it going down,' another girl said. 'You know – creeping.'

Horace presently found himself back in the kitchen. Maude, who had the two Venetian jugs, the remaining bottle of wine and a fresh nosegay of mint in readiness on the table, greeted him with the long rattle of an ice-tray and the voice of a skele-ton:

'Oh! you're back, are you?'

A certain chill in the air was softened by the unexpected discovery by Horace that he was still holding the glass of gin and tonic in his hands. He drained it gratefully.

'No more brandy,' Maude said, in a tersely detached voice,

rather as if it were his fault, 'and the *maraschino*'s nearly all gone. But I found some *Kirsch*. Cherry, isn't it? Tommy brought it from Germany once. Will it do?'

Horace didn't know and suddenly, impelled by gin mixing itself with wine-cup, didn't care. He started shovelling cubes of ice into a jug. Popular, was he? He poured generous measures of *Kirsch* over the ice and stirred madly with a spoon. Popular? Peals of laughter coming from across the lawn made him pause abruptly and gaze through the window. The garden was bright with chattering, wine-flushed girls.

'Seem to be enjoying themselves,' Horace said. 'Gay sight.'

Maude, otherwise speechless, gave a snort that clearly dismissed all other womenfolk as worse than pitiful. Horace, hardly noticing, pulled the remaining Moselle cork and tipped the bottle upside down, vertically, in a gesture meant to be expert. The neck of the bottle struck his gin glass, sending it crashing to the floor.

Unserene and highly silent, Maude swept up the broken glass with brush and dust-pan and then left the kitchen abruptly, in even higher silence, carrying with her a tray of strawberries and cream.

Left alone, Horace discovered that he was actually laughing to himself. Popular, eh? It was getting to be rather fun. Popular? He stirred with joyful energy at the nearly completed cup, raising a veritable sonata from the ice as it went swirling round and round. An over-generous squirt of soda sent the level of liquid too high in the jug and suddenly it was all brimming over. Horace, laughing to himself again, remedied the situation by pouring himself a generous glass of wine-cup and then tasting it deeply. Not bad at all, he thought. Not bad. Small wonder it was popular. The *Kirsch*, allied to *maraschino*, had undoubtedly given it a remarkably bizarre and haunting flavour.

After giving the jug its final garnish of mint he bore it back to the drawing-room, now three parts empty. One of the girls, elderly by any standards, was holding trembling court in a corner by the fireplace, listened to by Mrs Sanders and three others, who now and then responded by laughing sweetly and bobbing up and down, like puppies.

Another, crowned by a precious piece of millinery in black velvet, dancing bits of jet and what seemed to be the hind part of a vermilion cockatoo, suddenly bore down on him as from some secret hiding place, saying:

'Ah! Ha, ha. I've caught you.'

A smoked sprat, speared on the end of a silver fork, waved merrily in front of his face.

'The pageant, wasn't it? I've been drilling my brain all morning trying to remember. You haven't forgotten, have you?'

Horace had hardly begun to protest that he had indeed forgotten when the waving golden sprat cautioned him, with the accompaniment of laughter as thin as a tin-whistle, not to be silly. Of course he hadn't forgotten.

'Gorgeous day, that. I ran a fish-for-the-bottle stall. You won nearly every time. You knew the knack. I knew you did. I knew all the time you knew the knack, but I wouldn't split. You did know, didn't you?'

A moment later the sprat described a smart elliptical dive in the air and fell on the floor. Horace, hastily setting down the jug of wine-cup on a side-table, rushed to pick it up, holding it by its tail.

'Well, that's the end of that.' The precious piece of millinery suddenly disdained all connexion with the sprat. 'I hardly knew what it was for, anyway.'

'You mean you don't want it?'

Horace, left suddenly alone, turned to dispose of the sprat by dropping it into a vase of irises but then thought better of it. At the same time he recalled the excellence of the fresh-made cup and told himself that now was as good a time as any to sample it again. But before he could pick up the jug the peremptory hands of his sister had snatched it away and the bullying voice was at him again:

'Where on earth have you been? They're all panting with thirst outside. And what's that in your hand?'

Phoebe Hooper actually pushed him through the open french windows and into the garden. It was blissfully warm outside and her voice was jagged as glass as it nagged him about his duty and the way he had neglected it. He wondered how and where he had failed and, still holding the sprat by its tail, wondered equally what on earth he should do with it. He made as if to throw it casually into a bed of pansies but at once she positively flew at him:

'Not in there. That's disgusting. Put it in your pocket or something.'

He dutifully put the sprat in his pocket. He then remembered Miss La Rue and how much she wanted to talk to him and that it was his urgent duty to take her another glass of the cup.

He hurried back into the house for glasses, only to be met on the threshold by Maude, bearing another tray of strawberries and cream. She made way for him in silence; their paths might never have crossed; she was a cold stranger a thousand miles away.

In the corner of the drawing-room the elderly girl and her court were all eating strawberries and cream, bending closely over their plates like lapping puppies at their dinners.

Horace picked up a pair of empty glasses and started to pursue his sister across the lawn. The girls were scattered everywhere in the sun and now in his haste he half ran into one of them. Solitary and confined as if by an invisible wall of glass Dodie Sanders held him for the swiftest moment in too exquisite embarrassment, eyes dropping into excruciating shyness a moment later.

Something made him say: 'You haven't got a glass,' but a moment later she timidly lifted one containing a thimbleful of sherry, as if from somewhere up her sleeve. The smile on her face was wan; the three words she dropped were a ghostly trinity of whispers:

'Quite all right –'

Disturbed, and with some of his own shyness unaccountably returning, Horace was about to tell her that he would be back in a minute with more sherry when Phoebe Hooper, accusing him yet again of slacking about and doing nothing when everybody was dying of thirst, thrust the Venetian jug into his hands and flew away.

He paused to look at Dodie Sanders. The lids of her eyes quivered and fell again. She looked for a moment like a fish embalmed in the centre of a dazzling aquarium of aimless light.

'Have you tried my cup?'

No, the droopy lips confessed, she hadn't – she –

'Try it.'

Horace waited for her to drain her glass of sherry. He thought he actually saw her start to smile, and then think better of it, as he poured a little of the cup for her.

'Did you try the first lot?' he said. 'This is different. Would you hold my glass? I'd like a drop myself. No harm in the barman having –'

Eyes downwardly fixed on the two glasses, she was utterly silent as Horace poured wine-cup from the jug. The interlude, Horace thought, was almost like a dreamy doze after all his hectic travellings between kitchen and garden, with Maude and his sister and the various girls at his heels, but he woke suddenly to hear:

'Popular man, popular man. Can't have you being cornered.' Miss Tompkins, laughing frivolously, caught his arm and started to pilot him away. He had just time to grab his glass from Dodie Sanders and take a hurried drink at it before she set him fully on his course. 'Miss La Rue was one of those who was asking –'

He moved about the lawn, topping up glasses. A group of five girls, standing by a magnolia that had only recently shed the last of its blossom in big ivory curls, were clearly telling stories of doubtful character, he thought, and a hush like a strait-jacket encircled them tightly as he arrived.

One by one they all refused the cup. They were all ginny girls, they said. Eyes much reddened, they laughed with un-seemly pleasure into his face as he prepared to retreat with jug and glasses, but just before he turned his back one called to him with arresting winsomeness:

'I'll have a spot. I'll try it. They all tell me it's been 'normously popular.'

A well-built girl of seventy, with hair as light as the head of a seeded dandelion, came forward to capture him with a pair of violet eyes brimming over with alcohol. A pair of heavy garnet ear-rings dangled against her neck. The front of her carmine dress was low. Her bosom, unusually white, exposed itself like the upper portions of a pair of wrinkled turnips. She gazed down on it with the most possessive and flirtatious of glances, all the creases of her neck quivering like crumpled lace, and said, laughing:

'One man and his jug, eh? Well, let's try it.' Horace, now laughing too, the word popular again dancing mystically in his ears, poured wine-cup into his own glass – it was important to keep the other one, he thought, for Miss La Rue – and the well-built girl drank with heartiness, telling him:

' 'Licious. Absolutely 'licious. Can't think why you didn't come before. Nice to share your glass –'

She gave it back to him, empty. The possessive and inviting glance that she had previously reserved for her own bosom was now suddenly turned on Horace. She muttered a few low, amorous words about his big, brown eyes, at the same time gazing into them, and Horace glowed.

'Got to do the rounds!' he suddenly told her in an amazing burst of abandon. 'Customers everywhere.' An abrupt turn of the heel caused him to stagger slightly. 'Too damn popular, this stuff. That's the trouble.'

' 'Licious. 'Bye,' she said. She waved a hand infantile in its spidery fluttering, her seedy violet eyes overflowing. 'Quite 'licious –'

He went in search of Miss La Rue. He found her beyond the azaleas, alone, sitting on a white iron seat against the trunk of a vast acacia. Although she sat with grace, legs crossed, she had allowed the skirt of her costume to ride up, exposing a shapely silken knee. A delicate and bewitching smile accompanied her invitation to Horace to come and sit close to her. She actually patted the seat an inch or two from her thigh, affectionately scolding him at the same time:

'You've been naughty. Where have you been? You neglected me.'

Horace protested that he had been rushed off his feet. The cup had taken some time to make and there were customers everywhere.

'Nonsense. You've been flirting again.'

'My goodness, no.'

'I saw you. I watched you from here. First Miss Sanders and then the creature in the red dress.'

From somewhere behind the acacia a fountain tinkled. Its bright and spirited notes might have been Horace's own responses to Miss La Rue's flattering, warming words.

'Well, now that you're here you might at least give me some cup. Of course if you're too engrossed in looking at my knee –'

'Oh! I'm sorry. I'm so sorry.'

'Oh! I don't mind.' She turned the knee delicately from side to side, appraising it. I'm rather proud of it. Not at all bad, I think, do you?'

'Well, certainly it –'

'Don't be afraid. You were going to say for a woman of my age, weren't you?'

Horace, embarrassed, started to pour out the remainder of the wine-cup, at the same time making apologetic noises intended to indicate that he couldn't agree with her at all.

'Oh! yes you were,' she said. 'The trouble is you've no idea how old I am, have you?' Not waiting for an answer, she raised her eyes to the sky, wonderfully remote and ethereal in its clear blue spaciousness beyond the little white flowers of the gigantic acacia. 'I am a little older than the tree – the acacia, I mean. It's eighty-five. I know to the day. I remember it being planted.'

It was on the tip of Horace's tongue to pay her an immediate compliment but shyness overcame him again and he stopped in the middle of his opening syllable.

'Well?' she said.

'Oh! nothing, nothing.'

I thought for a moment you were going to flatter me.'

'Oh! no, no.'

'How disappointing,' she said. 'I hoped you were.'

Glass in hand now, she moved more closely to him, squeezing his elbow gently with her free hand. She drank, raising miraculously bright eyes to the summer sky.

'You've been experimenting with the cup.'

Horace, once again engrossed in the shining silken knee, confessed that as a matter of fact he had. It had been forced upon him.

'*Kirsch*,' she said. She drank again and smacked her lips appreciatively, with the utmost delicacy. 'And a touch of *maraschino*. Strange combination but clever of you. Fill me up.'

She gave him a flattering and vivacious glance and he filled her up, at the same time topping his own glass too. Freed of his sister and the chattering demands of the girls, Horace was beginning to feel absolutely splendid again. Clever, was he? Popular? Popular and clever! Ah! well, the party was terrific too. He was very glad, after all, that he'd come. He was just the chap to have around at a party. All the girls appreciated him.

He drank again and Miss La Rue moved closer. All the warm intoxication of the summer day seemed suddenly to descend like a pillar of light fire from heaven and Horace gave the exposed shining knee a long look, covetous and almost idolatrous at the same time.

Miss La Rue was quick to notice it and beguiled him further by saying:

'Go on. You may squeeze my knee if you want to.'

Horace, freshly flushed with wine-cup, started to protest that nothing was further from his mind but she merely laughed, mocking him slightly.

'Don't be silly. You've been wanting to for some time.'

The beginnings of an outrageous fire started to dart about Horace's veins. He felt himself drawn with irresistible force to the knee and suddenly, with an impulse of considerable abandon, started caressing it.

'It's perfectly all right,' she said with a light coolness that was also slightly mocking. 'Don't be afraid. No one's watching.'

Horace, encouraged, squeezed the knee with relish, at the same time laughing a little tipsily. Miss La Rue laughed too and pressed the side of her face close to his ear, the little veil of her hat touching and slightly tickling him. The whisper she gave him a moment later might have been a thunderclap of emotional surprise:

'It isn't the first time it's been squeezed. Nor, I hope, the last.'

'No?' Horace said exultantly. 'No?'

The noise of the fountain ran thrillingly in his ears, to be echoed suddenly by the notes of a blackbird almost bursting its breast in song somewhere at the very pinnacle of the acacia tree.

'You do it rather well, too,' she said.

'My God,' Horace said all of a sudden, 'you must have been absolutely great when you were young!'

Instantly she regarded him with sly petulance, eyes bright with overtones of mocking reproval.

'After that remark,' she said, 'I think I should take my leave.'

'Oh! no, no. Please,' Horace said. He felt suddenly reduced to the proportions of a small boy again. 'I didn't mean – no, please –'

'Up to that moment you'd been very tactful.'

'Oh! no please –'

'It was heaven sitting here under the acacia and you went and spoilt it all.'

'Now, really, listen –'

'You wouldn't say a thing like that to the tree, would you? My tree, I mean.'

'Yes, but that's different –'

'How?' she said. She gave him a glance of flirtatious severity, at the same time lifting his hand from her knee rather as if she were lifting up the arm of a gramophone. 'The acacia is far more beautiful now than the day it was planted.'

'So are you,' Horace said. 'So are you. I mean –'

'It's all very well to say that now.'

'Yes, but I mean it.' In an effort to exert physical as well as moral pressure Horace again put his hand on her knee. She moved it away at once, with a gesture aloof and almost prudish.

'Oh! look, we were getting on so well –'

'We were indeed. In fact I was thinking of letting you –'

'Letting me what? Letting me what?'

'It's too late now.'

'Oh! what was it?' Horace said. 'Please.'

'I was thinking of letting you kiss me.' She smiled teasingly.

'My hand, of course.' To Horace's dismay and astonishment she drained the last of her wine-cup, gave him the glass and actually stood up. 'But it's too late now. You can kiss Miss Sanders instead.'

'Miss Sanders?' Either he or she was going mad, Horace thought. 'Miss Sanders? Why on earth Miss Sanders?'

'Because she's coming this way. She's looking terribly soulful. She's obviously looking for someone like you to talk to.'

Horace turned his head to see, coming from the direction of the flaming azaleas, the wandering Dodie Sanders. Alone and shy, she seemed about to turn away when Miss La Rue waved her hand and called:

'Dodie. Come over and sit down. Mr Hooper's dying to talk to you.'

'Don't,' Horace said. 'Don't. Please. Don't.'

'Don't be silly. She's charming when you get to know her.'

'I don't want to get to know her.

'Don't be unkind. She's a girl who needs company.'

'But not mine, for God's sake.'

'Don't talk like that. It's tactless.' She gave him a maddening smile of mocking intimacy, with the added pain of a slight touch on his arm. 'Of course you're very young. You'll learn better as you grow up.'

Speechlessly, crushed and in positive pain, Horace watched the arrival of Dodie Sanders as if she were chief mourner at the sudden and cruel demise of the summer morning. He was no longer aware of the thrilling voices of the fountain and the blackbird.

'Come along, Dodie dear. Sit down,' Miss La Rue said. Once again the polished curve of her chin caught for a moment a reflection of sunlight as on a shell. Her neat light figure, belying all its years, turned away with grace and poise. 'There's a little of Mr Hooper's wine-cup left. You can have my glass. Mr Hooper will wash it out in the fountain, won't you, Mr Hooper?'

She walked away, airily, a moment later. When she had gone Dodie Sanders sat down on the seat, Miss La Rue's empty glass in her hands.

'Give it to me and I'll wash it,' Horace said.

'Oh! please don't bother.'

'It's no trouble.'

'Oh! please don't bother.'

After that Dodie Sanders stared, in complete silence, at the distances. Across the lawn some of the girls were drifting away in groups or in ones and twos. The casual uplift of semi-distant voices only seemed to deepen the pall of silence that hung between Horace and the shy Miss Sanders, who sat twisting the empty glass in her hands.

'My Heavens it's hot,' Horace said. A long and intolerable interval of utter silence had left him constrained and sweating. 'I really think I shall have to go in.'

A moment later he took out his handkerchief to mop his forehead and as he did so the smoked sprat fell to the ground.

For almost half a minute Dodie Sanders gazed down at it with uninspired gravity. Once she lifted her head and stared up into the acacia tree, as if thinking perhaps that the sprat might mysteriously have dropped from there.

'Where did that come from?'

'It fell out of my pocket.'

'It's one of those sprats, isn't it?'

Horace said it was. After another silence of considerable length, during which Horace suffered himself to be tortured by a vision of Miss La Rue's brilliant ageless eyes seemingly doting on him to a mocking chorus of fountain and blackbird, she made a remark so astonishing that it reduced him to a profound and impotent silence too.

'In a way sprats are rather beautiful,' she said, 'aren't they?'

Horace squirmed; he uttered, mentally, a protesting 'Blast!' And suddenly, as if the imposition of yet another awful silence were not enough, he heard a familiar goading voice driving across the lawn:

'Horace! Time to go! We're departing!'

'My sister,' he explained. 'I'm afraid I'll have to say good-bye –'

He fled across the lawn. Hastily he bore the Venetian jug and the last dregs of its wine-cup out of the deep acacia shade, past the flaring azaleas, across the lawn and through the drifting procession of departing girls. A late glimpse of Miss La Rue getting nimbly into a black limousine aroused an echo so searing that he uttered, aloud this time and almost involuntarily, another monumental 'Blast! and blast again!'

'What's the matter with you?' Phoebe Hooper said. 'Didn't you enjoy the party? I thought it was you who was the great success?'

'Of course he was, of course he was.' Miss Tompkins, in almost passionate assertion, waved delighted and almost tipsy hands to the sky. 'He was like the weather. He was wonderful. He improved all the time he got better.'

Half an hour later the lawn was empty. The heat of early afternoon had already woven a hush so deep that each waternote from the fountain beyond the acacia tree could be distinctly heard in a separate crystal fall. The only figures to be seen now were those of Maude and Miss Tompkins, occasionally darting into the garden to pick up a glass, and the solitary figure of Dodie Sanders, silent under the old acacia, staring down at the fallen sprat, golden at her feet.

She alone did not seem to realize that the party for the girls was over.

The Cat who Sang

WILFRED WHITMORE, who was exceptionally fond of music and taught Latin and Greek at a local school for boys, had overworked himself so much during the hot summer term that he began, about the middle of August, to suffer from odd hallucinations.

Once he believed himself, very briefly, to be Octavius Caesar and that he was eating large quantities of green figs and snails under the shade of an enormous cedar tree. Another time he was a Greek athlete, always in pursuit of other athletes or running away from them, along cruelly brilliant, stony distances.

Finally, after a too heavy lunch of sausages and mashed, fried onions and apple pie and cream, he fell asleep at his flat, in an old rocking chair, to wake suddenly under the powerful impression that his cat Susie was actually singing Schubert's *Die Forelle*, *The Trout*, or at least that particular passage in it that starts

At first he thought that this was merely part of a waking dream but when he at last sat up and heard with amazed and fully awakened ears Susie's unmistakable rendering of the song he was so excited that he rushed straight to the telephone without thinking there was anything absurd about the whole affair and immediately rang his fiancée, Shirley Baines, who worked as secretary to the general manager of a local paint factory.

Miss Baines, who was hard at it in the middle of an unbearably hot afternoon, typing letters and desperately longing for a stir of breeze to drive some of the acrid odour of emulsion paints from the humid air, was not particularly pleased to be interrupted.

'But she sings, I tell you. No mistaking it. Positively sings.'

'Who on earth are you talking about?'

'It was just after two o'clock. I'd given her a nice lunch and suddenly she sat up and started. Clear as a bell. Just as if she'd learnt it all off by heart.'

'For goodness' sake can't you tell me who you're talking about?'

'Susie. Didn't I say Susie?'

'No, you didn't. And what's more I don't like being interrupted at the office. I've told you before –'

'What makes it all the more exciting is that she doesn't just sing any old piece. She's shown taste – it's that awfully nice thing of Schubert's, *The Trout*, the bit that goes like –'

Wilfred suddenly began to hum over the telephone, in a rather uncertain tenor, the relevant passage from the song. At the end, trying to round off with a few bars of the accompaniment, he gave what seemed to be a series of hiccups, so that Miss Baines had great difficulty in restraining an impulse to ask him how long he'd been drinking. She remembered in time that Wilfred never drank and she could only suppose that the unbearable heat of the afternoon had in some way affected him. He'd been a little strange lately.

'And it wasn't as if she sang it just once. Then I *might* have been mistaken. But she sang it three times – two encores, note for note the same.'

'In the right key too, I suppose?'

'Absolutely.'

'Of course you'll put her on television at once.'

Something in the tone of Miss Baines' voice jolted his enthusiasm sadly.

'You sound a bit peeved. Don't you believe me?'

'Of course I do. Tomorrow you'll be telling me she plays the trombone. What's the matter with you? You must have been sitting out in the sun. You've been acting a bit odd lately –'

'I have not been sitting out in the sun.'

'Then what's the matter with you? It all sounds terribly fishy to me.'

In cold, level tones Wilfred said that if that was her idea of a joke he didn't think it was a particularly good one.

'And I can't say I think it much of a joke to be rung up in the middle of a scorching afternoon to be told about cats singing Schubert.'

'It is not a joke. It's deadly serious. Don't you realize? Susie's a singing cat. A phenomenon. I've got a phenomenal, wonderful creature on my hands.'

'Well, you haven't got me on them, because I've got work to do and if I don't do it I'll be here all night.'

'Very well. Will I see you tonight?'

'I thought that was the idea.'

'Perhaps you'll come to the flat and hear Susie sing?'

'If she's still at it I will. In the meantime you'll probably find she's got a bone stuck in her throat or something and it's that what's causing it – Good-bye.'

'Good-bye, Wilfred said and then in a sudden spasm of anxiety rushed to the kitchen, half afraid that Miss Baines' painfully jocular words might be true. But to his great relief Susie was asleep under the table, a passive ball of smooth black fur.

'They don't believe us, Susie,' he said. 'They don't believe about you. But I'm sure Schubert would have. And so will they. I'll make them.'

Back in the office Miss Baines tried vainly to repress the rising edges of her temper. She felt as if a hot iron had been run over her neck and she at once made several mistakes on the typewriter. Her hands felt repulsively clammy as she worked with her india-rubber to erase the misspelt words.

Finally she gave the typewriter a bang of near exquisite anger, snatched up her handbag and went first to the washroom to rinse her hands and make up her face and then down to the first floor canteen to get herself a drink of something cool.

'Hullo. You look as if you've been having a dust-up with somebody. Robbie?'

Dawn Edwards, who changed the colour of her hair twice a month, sometimes to a deep-sea blue or to a shade rather like that of an under-ripe tomato, sat at a plastic-topped table sipping at a glass of cold milk. Robbie was Mr Robertson, the general manager. Miss Edwards was secretary to a Mr Watt-

Forbes, whom she called Old What-not, in accountancy. Today Miss Edwards' hair was a strange shade of gold-green, rather like that seen in certain mosses after a dry summer.

'Robbie's gone swimming, lucky devil. I'd give something to be in that water.'

'I wish Old What-not would take a dive. He never lets up. Who were you fighting with?'

Miss Baines, who was now sipping cold orange juice, explained that she'd been fighting with Wilfred, over the telephone. It had made her very cross too.

'Not like you two, is it? You don't often have dust-ups.'

'No. But this was plain ridiculous.'

Miss Edwards thought for a moment, staring at Miss Baines' hair, which was a pleasant natural shade of dark brown, and then said she thought it mightn't be a bad idea if she tinted it for a change – say red or cocoa. It was wonderful what a change of colour did to men. They started to look at you in quite a different way.

'He's gone completely barmy about a cat. Completely off his rocker.'

'In what way?'

'It sings.'

Dawn Edwards started laughing, rather shrilly.

'Oh! they all do that. I hear them all night long on the roof next to ours. You want to throw cold water on them.'

'This one's different. It sings Schubert.'

'Oh! classical. No rock 'n roll?'

'Nothing so common. And he made such a God-Almighty fuss about it too. I never heard of anything so ridiculous.'

Miss Edwards pondered again, staring hard at Shirley's hair. A nice shade of light cocoa would do a lot for it, she thought.

'I don't know that it's so ridiculous. After all they get dogs to count. I saw one once on television.'

'There's a big difference between barking a few times and singing Schubert's *The Trout* in the right key.'

'Yes, but they get elephants to dance in circuses and all that. That must be difficult. And what about those porpoises or whatever they're called? They're almost human.'

Miss Baines suddenly drained her orange juice and said she must get back to the grindstone, or she'd be there till the cows came home.

'The thing that made me feel so mad was that you'd think the wretched animal was far more important than I was.'

Dawn Edwards laughed again and said that a situation like that called for something drastic. She urged Shirley once again to do something for her hair: say a nice cocoa or squirrel red or milk chocolate or something of that sort.

Two hours later, when Miss Edwards left the office, sharp on five, she was surprised to see Wilfred Whitmore standing outside the paint factory gates, waiting for Shirley Baines. Wilfred was very thin and tall and rather fragile of appearance. She thought he looked tired. His skin looked rather like greasy parchment and his longish blonde eyebrows were so pale as to seem almost as if dipped in salt.

'Oh! Wilfred, I've been hearing about your marvellous cat.'

'You have?'

'I think it's terrific. No wonder you're excited.'

'You mean you actually think Susie *can* sing? You don't think it's a joke?'

'Of course I don't. As I said to Shirley they get dogs to count numbers and all that. And you see elephants dancing to tunes. And bears. And you can get budgerigars to say anything.'

Wilfred said he could quite see that at first sight it seemed a little far-fetched that a cat should suddenly start singing, and Schubert at that, but when you thought about it a bit it really wasn't. After all there'd long been a theory that cats were in some way the reincarnation of human beings – it was what made them so close to man and so sagacious – and who could say whether Susie wasn't in fact a reincarnation of someone who had lived in Vienna in Schubert's time? Perhaps a person of some eminence, above the common rut; perhaps one of Schubert's friends?'

Miss Edwards' eyes, which were a sort of golden toffee colour, seemed almost to melt as she listened to this theory and she could think of nothing to say except:

'And of course she could always have heard it on a record.'

'Yes, of course. Why not? I'd never thought of that.'

At this moment some instinct made Miss Edwards turn her head, just in time to see Shirley Baines leaving the front door of the office. With the lightest of fingers she touched the side of her mossy hair and gave Wilfred Whitmore a final gaze with her buttery golden eyes, saying:

'Anyway I'd love to hear her some time.'

'You honestly would? Really?'

'Of course. I'd adore it. It would be marvellous.' She smiled with sudden beatific warmth, so that Wilfred was momentarily embalmed in a daze. 'Whenever it's convenient, I mean. Well, I must rush now.'

'I'll let you know. I'll let you know.'

After a bare, brief hullo to each other Wilfred Whitmore and Miss Baines walked away from the paint factory, silently. The white pavements seemed to dance with heat. Miss Baines felt herself longing for an ice-cream as big as a clock tower and for somewhere cool to swim.

'You didn't say you were coming to meet me out.'

'No, but I wanted to go to the fishmonger's for Susie and I thought I'd do the two things together.

A burst of fury rushed through Miss Baines. Her words were drops of strychnine.

'Of course you've bought her trout.'

Wilfred felt himself bounce off the pavement. For fully half a minute he seemed to soar somewhere far away from Miss Baines, floating in an icy sky. At the same time he suddenly recalled Dawn Edwards, her warm enthusiasm for Susie and the friendliness, almost the fondness, of her buttery golden eyes.

'Look, I know you're sceptical about all this. I know you don't believe me. All I ask is that you should come back to the flat and hear Susie for yourself. She's sung the same passage five times again already this afternoon.'

'Thanks. There's only two things I want at the moment. A good long cold drink or an ice and somewhere to swim.'

'I've got plenty of drink and plenty of ice at the flat and you can have a shower.'

'All right. Let's get it over with. Don't let's keep the prima donna waiting.'

At the flat Miss Baines declined the offer of a shower and merely sat in the living room with an air of martyred discomfort, in the rocking chair, sipping a large gin-and-tonic from a frosty glass. Susie was still in the kitchen.

'I won't bring her in till she's finished her supper. She seems to do it better after food.'

'Unlike most other singers.'

'Oh! and by the way I rang up the vet and told him all about it. He says he's never heard of a phenomenon like it and he's coming round first thing tomorrow to have a good look at her vocal cords.'

'Oh! ridiculous. It's probably croup or some sort of disease.'

'Well, it may be. We don't know. After all tenor-singing is a sort of disease.'

'Oh! is it? I never heard.'

Five minutes later, after charging Miss Baines' glass, Wilfred went into the kitchen and brought back Susie, who seemed dazed, even dopy, from too much food

Miss Baines applauded the entrance pertly

'Oh! don't do that. You'll put her off.'

'It's the usual thing to applaud the artist, isn't it?'

'Yes, but not this one. Just let her alone. Let her take her time. She'll do it in her own good time.

Miss Baines laughed shortly, in rather a gritty sort of way.

'I suppose she isn't expecting kittens or anything? Then we could have a choir.'

Wilfred could find no answer to this and sat in deeply repressed silence, watching Susie, who was now sitting on a sofa and licking her paws and reflectively washing her face with them. In impatience Miss Baines tinkled the ice sharply against the side of her glass, disturbing Susie, so that she looked quickly up.

'Sssh! Don't move. She's going to start.'

Suddenly Susie began to make strange sounds, at first *sotto voce*, then more loudly, on a rising, piercing scale. The inharmonious nature of the notes seemed utterly to fascinate

Wilfred Whitmore, who sat enthralled, open-mouthed, eye-brows seemingly bristled with excitement, his two hands gently beating enthusiastic time.

'There it is. That's it. That's the Schubert bit.' His voice was the merest thistledown of a whisper. 'Dah! – dah! – dah dah! – hear it? That's *The Trout*.'

To Miss Baines the sounds were like the unbottled echoes of distant caterwaulings on cold moonlight nights. She longed to hurl the contents of her glass at Susie, who seemed to be in mortal pain. Instead she drained the contents of the glass herself, slammed the glass down on the top of Wilfred Whitmore's upright piano and got up.

'I've just about had enough of this nonsense. I'm off. You're heading for a nervous breakdown.'

'Now don't go. Don't rush off. Give her a chance. She's only just started. That was just a sort of dummy run.'

'Dummy, my foot. You'll be telling me next she knows the difference between a diminished fifth and a cork leg –'

'Look, I'm convinced the root of all this lies in some sort of reincarnation.'

'Oh! you are? Well, I'll tell you what. You get the vet to look at you in the morning. Not her.'

'Now please. Don't rush off like that. Will I see you tomorrow?'

Miss Baines abruptly left without an answer. The door of the flat slammed with a cold rattle – a sound that Wilfred Whitmore felt he could still hear as he paced up and down outside the gates of the paint factory at lunch-time next day.

'Oh! it's you, Mr Whitmore. I thought for a moment it couldn't possibly be. We don't often see you at lunch-time.'

He turned to see Dawn Edwards, who had been wondering most of the morning what colour she should dye her hair next. She was getting rather tired of the golden-green.

'You've no idea when Shirley might be coming out to lunch, I suppose?'

'She's taking lunch late today. Mr Robertson's dictating letters till two o'clock. He wants to get away early for the weekend.'

Wilfred Whitmore's face seemed sad, even depressed, at the news.

'You look rather down in the dumps. It isn't your cat, is it? How is she today?'

'Oh! she's very well, thank you.'

'Still singing?'

'As a matter of fact I think she's singing better than ever.'

'In really good voice, eh? How wonderful. I'd love to hear her. You did say I could some time.'

'Of course. By the way, I had the vet to her this morning.'

'And what did he say?'

'I don't think he's very musical. He didn't strike me as having much taste.'

'Oh! you never know with those fellows. They look at everything so scientifically.'

Miss Edwards' eyes seemed to melt as she said this. A sympathetic glow seemed to spread across her face, prompting Wilfred Whitmore to say:

'I don't know how you're fixed for time. I don't want to upset your lunch hour but it wouldn't take five minutes if you wanted to hear Susie now.'

'Oh! goodness, I'd love to.'

At the flat Wilfred Whitmore set Susie on a yellow cushion, in the middle of the sofa, and again she gently washed her face with her paws before suddenly beginning to make the strange *sotto voce* sounds, rising to a piercing crescendo, that had seemed to Shirley Baines like nothing more than the unbottled echoes of distant caterwaulings on cold moonlight nights.

This is exactly what they seemed like to Dawn Edwards too. She thought the noise too ghastly for words but she merely transfixed the black, crying figure of Susie with her melting buttery eyes and said:

'But it's beautiful. She's a soprano too.'

'You recognize the Schubert? You know the song?'

'Of course. I used to play it a bit at one time.'

'You did? You don't sing as well, I suppose?'

'I used to. I was in the school choir and then later –'

'If I played would you sing the Schubert? *The Trout*, I mean. It would be rather nice.'

'I couldn't today. I haven't got the time today.'

'What about tomorrow?'

'I've got to have my hair done tomorrow. It takes hours.'

'Well, Sunday then?'

Before answering him Dawn Edwards leaned down and began to stroke Susie's black soft fur with the back of one hand. Against the bright yellow cushion the blackness of the fur seemed of unusual depth and brilliance and she said:

'Do you like black? I mean not just in cats. I mean does it sort of do something to you?'

How could she possibly know? he thought. He would never have guessed she was a girl of such perception. She didn't look the type and he was delighted when she said:

'All right, Sunday then. If you're sure that's all right? I mean what about Shirley?'

'We haven't arranged anything for Sunday. And even if we had –'

'All right, let's make it Sunday. Make it the evening, shall we? About six.'

'About six. And I'm thrilled you've heard Susie. I'm thrilled you like her.'

'Like her?' Again the melting buttery eyes spread their warmth. 'If I sing it half as well I'll be satisfied.'

When she arrived back at the flat on Sunday evening, thirty-five minutes late, Wilfred Whitmore found it for some moments hard to recognize her. The head of mossy golden hair, lightly shot with green, had disappeared. The sensational glowing black mane that had replaced it had a passionate depth in it and a strange light that smouldered at the edges with a touch of midnight blue. It seemed even richer and softer than Susie's fur.

Throughout the evening Dawn Edwards alternately drank gin-and-tonic and sang, in a very light soprano, brief snatches of Schubert. Wilfred Whitmore caressed the notes of the piano with vibrant hands. The evening grew dark and finally, as he and Dawn Edwards sat on the sofa together, he found himself caught up in yet another momentary hallucination. It was that Susie was ever so gently caressing his face with her fur. It was some time before he discovered, with an explosive jolt of excitement, that it was really Dawn Edwards' black, sensational hair.

Dawn Edwards is now Mrs Whitmore. Miss Baines continues to work at the paint factory. There is a certain brittleness in her manner and a certain aloofness, almost hauteur, in her bearing. She becomes increasingly irritated by Mr Robertson and he, in turn, by her. In order to sleep at night she takes increasing doses of phenobarbitone which in turn, as time goes on, have a diminishing effect on her.

Sleeplessly she lies and thinks of Wilfred Whitmore, Susie and Susie's strange cold discords. There frequently runs through her mind the whole of *Die Forelle, The Trout* – of which she now has a gramophone record – and particularly that beautiful passage in it that starts

And over and over again, as she hears it and sees in imagination the trout turning in its rippling waters, she wonders why cats are so popular.

More especially those who sing.

The Trespasser

'GOOD gracious,' Aunt Leonora suddenly yelled, 'that damned cow's eating the lupins again!'

A moment later, gold spectacles prancing, she was rushing with revengeful haste through the open french doors of the sitting-room and into the garden, snatching up on her way out one of the many old ash-plants, gnarled as twisted parsnips, that she kept handy for the purpose of chastising trespassers, stray animals, tramps, idlers, salesmen and anyone else who might be standing about and up to no good in the process.

'Shoo, you beast! Get out of it! Cow, do you hear?'

I followed her immediately, searching the calm sunny borders of the June garden in vain for a single sign of any trespassing cow. I should have known that none ever came there, that they were as mythical as the marauding herds of deer that nightly threatened beetroot and bean-rows, bringing Aunt Leonora downstairs with beating sticks and flashing lanterns.

I saw instead a tubby, mild-looking man, with a white top-knot of hair and a very scrubbed pink complexion, who looked not at all unlike a round fresh radish, standing with an air of absent surprise on the edge of the lawn, beyond which large colonies of lupin rose in gold and purple spires. A floppy black umbrella, on which he was pensively leaning for support, gave him the estranged appearance of someone who had been unexpectedly dropped into the garden by parachute and did not know, in consequence, quite where he was.

Aunt Leonora, who was baggy and big-limbed and looked not at all unlike a rampaging cow herself, meanwhile rushed onward to enlighten him. It was still not clear to me whether, in her short-sighted way, she could distinguish between man and beast and I was half-horrified, a moment later, to see her brandishing the ash-plant with violent challenge in the direction of the tubby man, obviously in readiness to beat him furiously about the rump.

A providential turn of his body brought him face to face with

her, just in time. Undismayed, she yelled an instant demand to
know what had happened to that damned cow she had seen
trampling all over the place a couple of minutes before?

'It's yours, I suppose, isn't it? It would be!'

A look of almost ethereal surprise enveloped the tubby man
so completely that he stood there as if embalmed. The gravity
of things was evidently still not clear to him and when his
mouth finally opened it was merely to let fall a single hollow
word.

'Cow?'

'Yes, cow. A damned great red and white one. Chewing the
lupins. Trampling all over the place.'

'I –'

'They're always at it. They're in here every day.' It was a
blatant lie, though I am sure she was unaware of telling it.
'Trampling and gorging everywhere. Where's it gone to? One
can't grow a thing without its being chewed up like a – like a –'
Aunt Leonora made a questing search of the air for a suitable
damning word – 'like a field of tares!' she suddenly spat out.
The word tares, delivered with a final hiss, had a positive fire in
it and set the tubby man back another pace or two. 'Who are
you anyway? Take your cow home. You're trespassing.'

After a glare of stunning power had struck the little man like
a point of blank charge of shot he managed somehow to find
an answer.

'I rather thought I was in my sister's garden,' he started to
say, 'but –

It was a most unfortunate remark to have made and Aunt
Leonora at once seized upon it with peremptory scorn.

'That's a damn-fool thing to think,' she said. 'Sister? What
sister? Whose sister?'

The tubby man, looking about him with deepening apprehension, almost despair, said he was terribly sorry but he could
have sworn that this was *The Limes*. A flutter of repeated apolo-
gies ran from his lips in a muted scale, ending with the words
'even the lupins looked the same –'

'Good God, man, *The Limes*. You mean you belong to Old
Broody? Her? She's your sister?'

'Miss Elphinstone – yes, she's my sister.'

Aunt Leonora let out the rudest of snorts and said Good God, she'd never known that Broody had men in the family and then, as if the withholding of this family secret from her was a sort of unneighbourly crime, glared at him with furious disbelief, plainly thinking him a liar. There was something ironical in the idea of her accusing someone else of not telling the truth and the little man stuttered as he said:

'Oh! yes. There are three brothers.'

'Married?' She threw the awful word at him with typical point-blank candour, clearly determined that no second family secret should escape her.

'Oh! yes, we're all three married. In fact my eldest brother and I have each been married a second time.'

'Caught twice, eh?' she said.

Unabashed, she bared her big friendly teeth and laughed into the tubby man's face with an expansive crackle and then a moment later further confused him by turning sharply to me and saying:

'This is my nephew. He just called to bring me some aubergine plants for the greenhouse. Raised them himself. I'm mad about aubergines. Like them stuffed. Do you garden?' Before the tubby man could attempt an answer she glared at me again, baring big teeth, and shook the stick. 'You saw that damned cow, didn't you?' she said to me.

I started to say that I hadn't seen anything of the kind. Somewhere in the distant past a solitary wandering cow had so far trespassed as to reach its neck over the fence and take a few modest bites from a lilac bush. Since then Aunt Leonora's complex had developed from strength to strength and now rampaging cows were everywhere.

'I think it must have been this gentleman you saw,' I said. 'After all the light's very strong this morning –'

'What's it got to do with the light?' she said and suddenly hurled at me a dark accusation. 'Your eyes wander,' she said. 'I could hardly mistake a man for a cow, could I?'

I kept silent; spectacles seemed to do little or nothing for her acute short-sightedness, and I refrained from reminding her that once, on a misty September evening, she had mistaken me for a wandering deer as I returned from a mushroom trip and had struck me a number of severe blows about the elbows before I could stop her. Deer were worse than cows; she was convinced that they actually jumped the fences; they could gorge a whole garden in a night.

'On a long visit?' she said, once again taking the tubby man by surprise with that fresh, alarming candour of hers, 'or just here today and gone tomorrow?'

Startled again, he began to explain that he was here for a week and then, looking hastily at his watch, said that he thought he ought to be going. It was rather later than he thought; his sister was inclined to be particular about meal-times. He didn't want to upset her.

'Which one are you?' she said. 'Charley? Now I come to think of it I think I've heard Old Broody talk of Charley.'

'Oh! no, Charley's my elder brother. I'm Freddie.'

'Oh! you're Freddie, are you?' she said, rather as if there were some awful mistake about his birthright, and then suddenly turned on him a smile of such masterful charm, her big teeth positively glowing, that I could have sworn his face reddened a little further. 'Oh! yes, of course. I think I've heard Broody talk of you too.'

'Well, I must go. I must bid you good-morning. It was awfully silly of me about – you know – and I –'

'We were just having a glass of sherry and a piece of saffron cake,' Aunt Leonora said in the sweetest of voices, 'Would you care to join us before you go?'

It was another blatant lie; we had been doing no such thing; she was merely putting it on for the trespasser.

'I honestly think I ought to go –'

'Oh! Broody and her lunch can wait. I suppose it's *risotto* anyway?'

'How do you know?' he said. 'As a matter of fact it is *risotto*.'

'Oh! I gave her the recipe years ago. She always has it on Thursdays. She's no imagination.'

Back in the house I poured sherry into cut glasses at a

side-board and turned once or twice to see the tubby Mr Elphinstone's eyes blinking and winking sharply in their effort to re-focus themselves after the blinding outdoor light of noon. This gave him an air of fidgeting discomfort, or as if he were dying to ask a question that had been bothering him for some time. And presently the question came:

'It rather made me smile, you calling her Broody. What makes you call her that?'

Aunt Leonora, looking up from cutting saffron cake, which she was placing in slices on small pink china plates that made her almost masculine hands look far larger and clumsier than they really were, said:

'It's the way she walks. I say she always seems to have a clutch of eggs in her pants.'

Mr Elphinstone actually chuckled. You could see that he thought it rather apt. Still chuckling, he accepted a portion of cake from Aunt Leonora, but the chuckle died suddenly on his lips when she said with pungent vehemence:

'Your sister's an old flap-doodle. She's the sort of woman who you want to do things to. She seems to forget women are emancipated,' she said, as if this had anything to do with it.

If Mr Elphinstone had any thought of making a loyal and defensive protest about this accusative remark it was utterly useless: Aunt Leonora, in full cry again, gave him no time at all.

'You know what I mean?' she said. 'You must have met women you wanted to do things to?'

A number of interpretations of this interesting theme sprang quickly to my mind and I sensed that they might be springing to Mr Elphinstone's too. He sipped at his sherry swiftly and must have been wondering what sort of house he had trespassed into when Aunt Leonora, almost as if in an attempt to save him from further embarrassment said:

'I mean most of them should have been strangled at birth, shouldn't they? or sterilized or something?' The mere suggestion of these harsh and unconventional measures made Mr Elphinstone recoil. 'I suppose your wives were different, weren't they?'

'Well –'

'Is your wife staying with Old Broody too? How do they get on?'

Mr Elphinstone, who had been pensively gazing for some moments at a remarkable but useless collection of hunting horns, silver cups, animal claws and such trophies that Aunt Leonora always kept on or over the mantelpiece, now fixed his eyes on a large brass pestle-and-mortar and said that, as a matter of fact, his wife was not with him. She had passed away, he explained, some four or five years before.

With nothing more than a brusquely consolatory cough Aunt Leonora said she was very sorry to hear it and then turned to me and said 'Give Mr Elphinstone some more sherry,' as if this would do something to help sustain him in his loss.

'What do you feel about the sherry?' She shot the question at him point-blank, as always, in a sort of bark. 'Like it?'

'Oh! excellent. Excellent.'

'It's absolutely awful,' she said. 'It's plain muck. Don't drink it. We'd have done better to have the redcurrant wine. Get the redcurrant wine,' she said to me. 'We don't want to poison Mr Elphinstone, do we?'

I murmured that that would, perhaps, be rather drastic but I don't think she really heard.

'Bring the six-year-old,' she called to me instead, as I went out to the kitchen. 'That was a good year. I fortified it a bit that year – you can tell the difference.'

When I came back with the bottle of wine – it was exactly the same brilliant colour as the ripe berries themselves – Mr Elphinstone was just saying, as he gazed again at the hunting horns:

'I see that you hunt.'

'You don't see anything of the sort,' she said. 'I loathe it.' She glared at him sternly: her teeth were bared like an open trap. 'Do you?'

'Oh! no, no, no.'

'I love animals. I adore birds. A pair of fly-catchers arrived yesterday. They always arrive at this time, every year. Are you interested in birds?'

Mr Elphinstone confessed that he wasn't, very, and she glared at him with increasing sternness again. Mr Elphinstone, who must have felt that he couldn't seem to manage to say the right thing at all at any time, looked quite nervous, almost shaken, at these constant accusatory glares and I tried to take the edge off things by offering him a glass of wine. He accepted this with eagerness and an upward half-smile, the sort of smile that men often exchange when they feel that women are getting at them, and I half-winked in reply. At this he seemed, I thought, quite comforted.

'And don't wink,' she said. 'What there is to wink about I don't know.' Another dark accusative glare followed: 'It's always your eyes that give you away.'

'I was merely saying cheers to Mr Elphinstone,' I said, 'only in another way.'

'Well, then say cheers,' she said, 'without the appendices.'

'Cheers,' I said and Aunt Leonora said 'Cheers' too, at the same time fixing Mr Elphinstone with yet another severe glare through her flashing gold spectacles.

It couldn't possibly have occurred to Mr Elphinstone at this time that these constant glares were the inevitable result of her chronic shortsightedness – she simply had to glare in order to see objects at all – or that the very brusqueness of her candour meant that she was very fond of men. Her drastic measures for the proposed extermination of her sex were not accidental; she had been figuratively killing off flap-doodles like Old Broody for years, just as she had been chasing and chastising imaginary hordes of cows and deer from her precious pastures of lupins.

Just as he must have begun to feel that the consistent barrage of glares was becoming too much to bear she suddenly smiled at him with utter sweetness, the sort of sweetness that only bony, toothy women of her kind can muster, and said:

'Well, what do you think of the wine?'

Mr Elphinstone, who clearly wasn't going to be caught out on the subject of wine a second time, hesitated a moment before collecting his thoughts and then said:

'It's most refreshing.'

'It's damn good!' she barked at him. 'I'll tell you that. You won't get better.'

'I will say it's unusual. It has a certain quality.'

'No idea where I got the recipe for this from? No? The Black Forest.' She took a great gulp of wine, rolling it ripely round her tongue. 'I was on a walking tour there with a girl-friend, years ago. We came to this place not far from Kreuznach, the spa you know, near the Rhine. Just a farmhouse, but we liked it so much we stayed there a month. Splendid place. We got sozzled on this stuff every day.'

'Sozzled?'

The word sprang from the lips of the surprised Mr Elphinstone before he could stop it. Sherry and the first half glass of red-currant wine had made his face pinker than ever, so that he looked more and more like a round, sparkling radish freshly washed.

'You don't need more than a couple of good big glasses,' she said. 'It's far more potent than any of your fancy hocks.'

Two cuckoos, one chasing the other, both calling as they flew, went sailing over the garden a moment later and Aunt Leonora immediately jumped up and went over to the french windows on the chance of watching them. The midday light was glorious beyond her. The lupins, at their unsullied best, glowed like tremendous candles in the noonday sun.

'Just the day to drink this stuff,' she told Mr Elphinstone. 'Good to be alive. You can taste the berries in it – it's got that cool sharpness.'

I accepted this as a signal to fill up the glasses. She held out hers with alacrity but Mr Elphinstone professed a certain wariness, confessing that he didn't really drink at lunchtime.

'Good God, man, drink up,' she said. 'You've nowhere to go, have you?'

Mr Elphinstone was bound to say that he hadn't anywhere to go, particularly, and I took the opportunity of replenishing his glass to the top.

'A zizz in the garden, I suppose?' she challenged him. Zizz was a favourite word of hers.

'Zizz?'

'Forty winks,' she said.

She was still at the french windows, big and dominant against the sun, and suddenly she put her head outside sniffing significantly.

'Wondering if I could smell the *risotto.*'

This remark was nothing less than a piece of low corruption. I knew that it was uttered solely as a means of undermining Mr Elphinstone's morale and I saw him start distinctly. But much worse was to follow:

'I've got cold salmon today,' she said. As if the remark alone were not enough she gave another of those magnificently sweet, disarming smiles, her voice more airy than usual this time. 'I suppose I ought to go and make the mayonnaise. Although the fresher it's made, I think, the better.'

A confused Mr Elphinstone took a long drink of wine and then stared for some moments into his glass, clearly torn between departure and a dream of mayonnaise.

'By the way,' she said suddenly to me, 'you promised to go and gather the strawberries for me and you never did. Are you going to be a lamb and run down and get them?'

This was another blatant lie. No word whatever had passed between us about strawberries; I had no idea there were strawberries; but suddenly, on an unexpected and curious tangent of memory, Mr Elphinstone's question about Aunt Leonora's hunting sprang across my mind and I said involuntarily, aloud:

'By Heaven you do.'

'You what?' she snapped. 'What was that you said?'

'Nothing, aunt,' I said. 'I was just thinking aloud, that's all.'

'Well then, don't,' she said. 'It's a bad habit.' Yet another dark accusative glare followed: 'It's even worse than thinking with your eyes.'

After this I was determined, out of sheer obstinacy, not to hurry the strawberries and I deliberately poured Aunt Leonora, Mr Elphinstone and myself another glass of wine. As she received hers she said:

'You'll find a dish in the kitchen. I think they'd look awfully nice in the green one – you'll see it, the one with the pattern of vine leaves.'

I ignored this completely and stood sipping wine.

'Strawberries?' Mr Elphinstone said. 'You mean you actually

have strawberries already? I say, that's very early isn't it?'

'I grew them under cloches,' she said. 'You get them three or four weeks early.'

'How wonderful.' Pinker than ever, Mr Elphinstone looked at her for the first time with uninhibited if slightly unsteady admiration. A sort of rosy dew had settled on the lower lids of his eyes, like a sparkling distillation of the wine. 'I think that's absolutely marvellous.'

'Hadn't you better go?' she said to me. 'It'll take some little time and I –'

'Just going,' I said. 'Enough for how many?'

'Oh! don't be ungenerous,' she called to me as I went through to the kitchen. 'I mean – there are plenty.'

When I came back from the kitchen garden, twenty minutes later, bearing the dish of remarkably fat ripe strawberries, the sitting-room was empty. But a peal of laughter of Aunt Leonora's from the kitchen, followed by a short chorus from Mr Elphinstone, told me where to look.

'In the kitchen Aunt Leonora was coaxing a basin of mayonnaise to its final smoothness and Mr Elphinstone, now in his shirt sleeves and wearing a kitchen apron with a pattern of large red prawns all over it, was cutting up hard-boiled eggs into neat slices with a wire-cutter. Two glasses of redcurrant wine stood on the kitchen table and between them, on a rose-patterned dish, lay a very pleasant-looking portion of cold salmon, pink as Mr Elphinstone himself, surrounded by sprigs of parsley and palest green circles of cucumber.

'Guess what?' Aunt Leonora said.

I guessed at once, and correctly.

'Mr Elphinstone's going to stay to lunch,' I said.

'Yes, I rang Broody,' she said. 'I asked her too but she felt she couldn't waste the *risotto*.'

This, I was sure, was yet another blatant and scandalous lie and I looked her squarely in the eye about it. In reply she deliberately made her spectacles twitch and turned away in shameless and divine ignorance to her mayonnaise, dipping one little finger into it and then slowly licking it in bemused appreciation.

'If you've finished the eggs,' she told Mr Elphinstone, 'you could sugar the strawberries.' And then to me: 'Give Mr Elphinstone some more red-currant. He's earned another swig.'

It was a good idea, I thought, for all of us to have another swig, but when I came back from the sitting-room Mr Elphinstone had disappeared from the kitchen. I couldn't see him anywhere. Some moments later I observed a figure doing gymnastic exercises of a violent sort beyond the kitchen window. It was Mr Elphinstone, energetic as any athlete, wildly hurling a clothful of wet lettuce-leaves about his head like an Indian club, spraying drops of water everywhere.

He came back perspiring deeply, rosier, more radishy than ever.

'Good boy,' she said sweetly. He beamed. He might actually have been a boy, praised suddenly for some good and sporting deed, and perhaps that was how she saw him, because a moment later she told me:

'We're going to eat in the garden. It's just the day. Then afterwards Mr Elphinstone can lie in the hammock and have a zizz.'

'I must be getting along,' I said. 'Is there something else I could do before I go? Will you want another bottle of wine?'

'What do we say?' she said. There was something devilishly and deliberately familiar about that 'we' as she tossed it into the air. 'Will we want another? I think we will, won't we?'

'Anything you say!' Mr Elphinstone said, laughing with crackling merriment. Really rubicund now, he was tossing lettuce leaves into a glass dish with careless abandonment, rather as if they were useless lottery tickets. 'Anything you say.'

'I'll get another,' I said.

'Magnificent stuff,' Mr Elphinstone said. 'Absolute ambrosia.'

'Don't forget the gooseberries and the eggs when you go,' she called after me as I went into the cupboard under the kitchen to get the wine. 'They're on the table just outside the french windows. I have heaps. Don't forget.'

Having found the wine I couldn't resist asking, for the last time, if there was anything else I could do.

'What about the hammock?' I said.

'Oh! it's up. I used it yesterday. The night was so fine I didn't bother to take it down.'

'What about cushions?'

'You're awfully dutiful today.' This was really another dark accusation, deeply shot with suspicion. 'Oh! Mr Elphinstone will cope with the cushions, won't you, Mr Elphinstone? After all he's the one who's going to have the zizz.'

I took a last look from Aunt Leonora to Mr Elphinstone. He seemed, I thought, to be having a sort of zizz already. His eyes, now rolling, now dancing, seemed to be like two excited valves bubbling pinkish water. He was actually chewing with rabbity pleasure on the crisp heart of a lettuce, as on a pale green cigar, and his forehead was so covered in perspiration that I fully expected to see it steam.

'Well, I'm on my way,' I said. 'Don't go over-eating the strawberries. Have a lovely zizz.'

'Bless you, my boy!' Mr Elphinstone called, the lettuce heart dropping suddenly out of his mouth. 'Hope to see you many times again.'

I said I hoped so too and went away in rumination across the lawn, past the gold and purple spires of lupins, the ancient Blenheim apple tree where Aunt Leonora's hammock hung in shade and finally out through the wicket gate in the hedge over which so many imaginary cows, not to say deer, so often seemed to rear their trespassing horns: quite forgetting, as I did so, to pick up the gooseberries and the eggs.

It was in fact three hours before I went back to pick them up. By that time, I reasoned, Mr Elphinstone would long since have gone home to rejoin his sister: Aunt Leonora, if I were lucky, would be indoors, immersed in one of the numberless tasks the masterful energies of an emancipated woman so insatiably demanded, jamming gooseberries, preserving cherries, candying flowers, so that it might be possible for me to sneak in and out again without being mistaken, as Mr Elphinstone had been, for some trespassing, marauding cow.

But greatly to my surprise the hammock was still swinging gently to and fro in the deep shade of the apple tree, with Mr

Elphinstone inside it, having his zizz. In the hot June silence Aunt Leonora was sitting beside him, a protective ash-plant at the ready, her large angular frame uncomfortably perched on a rather small red camp stool, rocking him gently to and fro like a child. The look of drowsy beatitude on her face gave her an air of such protective tenderness that she looked utterly remote from the woman who had so sternly chased him, a few hours before, as a trespasser.

I was silently escaping down an avenue of raspberry canes when a peremptory wagging of the ash-plant called me back. I was still several yards from the hammock when she recognized me and, in the sternest of low whispers, greeted me with yet another dark accusation.

'What are you prowling about at? Skulking like a tramp. I caught one stealing cabbages off the compost heap the other day.'

'Mr Elphinstone looks remarkably comfortable,' I said.

'Don't disturb him,' she whispered. 'He's worn out. He insisted on helping wash up and then actually ran the sweeper over the sitting-room.' She showered on me the unexpected luxury of a toothy, angular smile. 'He did love the strawberries. He had four helpings, and then finished up the cream with a boudoir biscuit.' Mr Elphinstone stirred suddenly – I could have sworn with the buttonhole of one eyelid very slightly open – and gave the most kittenish of snores before settling back into the luxurious depths of his zizz. 'He's had such a good long sleep. Don't you think he looks just like a child?'

I didn't; I thought he looked just like a fat red radish, as in fact he still does.

I suppose it was inevitable that Aunt Leonora should have married Freddie Elphinstone. I suppose it is inevitable too that she always thinks of herself as the masterful partner, tirelessly energetic in organization, up at six in the morning, hardly ever at rest, battling ceaselessly with chickens, eggs, the garden and its fruits, repelling idlers, cows and trespassers and still telling, when it suits her purpose, those blatant innocent lies. I suppose too there is a great deal to be said for women of her kind, who feel themselves to be so strong that, out of a sort of powerful charity, they love to take the burden of things off the shoulders of weaker creatures.

I suppose too there is much, perhaps even more, to be said for pink, tubby little men like my Uncle Freddie, who always look like round fat radishes. Uncle Freddie never gets up for breakfast; he takes it in bed, with *The Times* and two other newspapers, at ten o'clock. At twelve he dresses, takes a walking stick, strolls two hundred yards to *The Duke of Marlborough*, drinks two whiskies, chats about the weather and walks home for lunch at one o'clock. At two o'clock Aunt Leonora insists on his having a zizz. Very occasionally, when he wakes up, he plays golf or goes fishing, but not if it's too hot or too windy or too wet or too cold. While he rests, Aunt Leonora, who adores more than anything brisk, healthy exercise in the fresh air, bicycles to the library, changes his books for him and hurries back so that he shan't be unduly idle between tea, for which she always serves two kinds of bread-and-butter, three of cake and scones and four of home-made jam, and suppertime. After supper she busies herself with essential tasks like pickling eggs or drying flowers for winter while Uncle Freddie drops into a doze from which she finally wakes him with a glass of red-currant wine, mulled in winter, and a homemade ginger biscuit.

How nice it must be to be mistaken for a trespassing cow and thence to achieve, with neither mastery nor struggle all your purposes – not the least of which must be the long quiet zizz, under a shady apple tree, on warm summer afternoons.

The Diamond Hair-Pin

FOR some weeks after he had first found the hair-pin on the wooden seat in the park Tom Wakeling kept it wrapped up in tissue paper in a table drawer at his lodgings. It was a perfectly ordinary hair-pin, though perhaps rather longer than usual, except that it carried with it, for a time, a strong scent of carnations.

A few strands of dark hair were still clinging to it when he first picked it up and it was they, together with the scent of carnations, that made him start wondering, at first casually and then so deeply that it became an obsession, what sort of woman had left it there.

Soon he was going back to sit on the same park seat every evening after his work in the drawing office was over. The seat was on the bank of a small lake where flocks of mallard, various other ornamental ducks, a few swan-necked geese and occasional sea-gulls fought and dived for scraps of food thrown in by visitors.

He liked to throw pieces of bread to the birds himself and as he sat there breaking it up in his fingers he also looked very ordinary: shy, scrubby-haired, his skin rather pasty, his eyes seemingly short-focussed, as if from long hours of concentration over the drawing board. His hands were in fact the only features about him that were at all unusual. The fingers were long and narrow and very white. Because of his work they were immaculately kept, every inch of them so unblemished that they too, like the hair-pin, might have been wrapped up at night in tissue paper and carefully laid away.

The obsession with the hair-pin got hold of him slowly but, having taken hold, soon had him locked in hopeless entrancement. A more communicative person might have told himself that girls didn't wear hair-pins like that any longer. Old ladies did, however, and it therefore naturally followed that nobody more exciting than an old lady throwing bread to the ducks could have lost the pin – it simply wasn't worth bothering about anyway.

But a mind as cautious, withdrawn and self-centred as his couldn't relinquish facts so easily. Just as he drew lines on a sheet of paper with minutest accuracy so he microscopically scrutinized the facts. And the facts were that old ladies didn't have black hair and, unless he was much mistaken, didn't use the scent of carnations either. It seemed patently obvious to him that an altogether younger, more exciting and possibly provocative person had dropped the pin from her hair.

It was after nearly a month of this cautious and earnest speculation that the impossibly idiotic notion of advertising the hair-pin in a newspaper first came to him – except that to his sort of mind the idea seemed neither idiotic nor impossible. When he came to measure the facts it was clearly no more unusual than four-fifths of the things people expounded in the personal columns of newspapers every day – the heart cries for loved ones to come home, the pleas for stray cats, pet mice and budgerigars to be returned to their heart-broken owners, the rewards offered for the recovery of lost trifles, the universal promise that, at last, all was forgiven.

But when he came to frame the advertisement – he would put it in an evening paper, he thought; it was the sort of thing that might catch the eye of a girl going home on a bus or a train – it wasn't so easy. He had to admit that *Found: one black hair-pin. Owner please communicate Box No. X* sounded pretty pointless. The only possible explanation a lot of people would find for it was that it was a message in some sort of code. It might be anything from an agreed signal between crooks that a bank was ripe for picking or a communication of immense secrecy between lovers.

Whatever interpretation people might put on it he was perfectly sure that he would get numbers of useless and stupid replies. And he didn't want that; he was perfectly serious about it all. He had even built up in the more cautious recesses of his mind an image of the sort of girl who had lost the pin. To him there was nothing strange about that; nor was there anything strange in nursing the hope that one day, somewhere, somehow, in some miraculous sort of way, he might meet her. A delightful experience might come out of it.

Even so he grasped the necessity of making his advertisement more specific and, if possible, more tempting. And finally he made it so and put it in the evening paper.

Found: Adelaide Park, evening of June 26, one diamond hair-pin. Owner please communicate earliest possible Box No. X.

He got only three replies. One was from a lady, clearly elderly and acidly irate, who reminded him tersely of the penalties of stealing by finding and why hadn't he advertised before? She didn't claim the pin. The second was from a firm of city jewellers who said that in their experience diamond hair-pins were of such rarity that they would consider it a great favour if they might have the privilege of inspecting this one.

The third was from a person named Aimée Vibert. She wrote to him in a rather laboured, long-lettered script on dark blue paper. She too, he thought, was evidently living in lodgings, since her address was c/o Miss A. Winter. She wrote:

'You do not describe the pin with any detail but I myself am sure it is the one I lost six months ago and have never seen since. It was given to me by my aunt for my fifteenth birthday just before the war.'

He was pleased about this letter, which he read over and over again before deciding how to answer it. It not only told him that his correspondent had an elegant-sounding, rather exciting foreign name, but also roughly how old she was. His calculations put her at thirty-five or thirty-six, a year or two younger than he was. He eventually wrote back:

'If you could spare the time to meet me I would be happy to bring the pin along so that you can identify it. Would it suit you to meet me in the park, say at 7 o'clock on Thursday, at the seat where I found the pin? It is the third seat along from the little kiosk on the north side of the lake. I shall be wearing a grey charcoal suit and in all probability will be carrying a paper-bag of bread which I shall bring for the birds.'

She replied to this, on the same kind of unusually dark blue paper:

'I am afraid I am not able to manage to meet you earlier than half-past seven, as my companion, Miss Winter, likes us to eat at half-past six. Otherwise I look forward to meeting you and making your acquaintance. Please don't forget the pin. It is rather precious to me.'

After he had read this second letter several times he suddenly held it to his nose, sniffing it in the hope of smelling carnations, but the paper gave off no scent of anything at all.

Half an hour before he was due to meet her rain began to fall in the lightest of summer showers. The fragrance of rain on dust filled the park as he walked across it under an umbrella, carrying the paper bag of scraps of bread and biscuit which he had saved from his tea.

Although the rain stopped a few minutes before half past seven the park seat was wet, so that he couldn't sit down. Instead he rolled up his umbrella, leaned on it at the edge of the lake and started to feed the ducks with scraps of food. He seemed to do this with an air of great casualness, though in reality the palms of his long hands were as wet as if he had held them out in the rain.

At a quarter to eight she was standing there beside him and he was sure at once that she was foreign She had straight light brown hair cut short and a sallow complexion that made her look as if she had been shut away somewhere for a long time. She was extremely plain but an extraordinary transparency in the eyes gave them a brilliance that made up for all lack of colour. She was astonishingly thin too and was wearing one of those stone-grey mackintoshes that have shoulder-flaps that protrude like ears, so that it looked several sizes too large for her.

'I'm Tom Wakeling. I suppose you could be the lady who has come about the hair-pin?'

'Yes. That is so.' She spoke very formally, in a hopeless sort of voice, with a marked accent. 'Good evening.'

'Good evening.'

He instinctively made as if to shake hands but succeeded only in rattling the scraps of food in the paper bag.

'I'm sorry it rained,' he said.

'I am sorry, too.'

'I'm afraid it's made the seats wet.'

'I'm afraid it has.'

'I think the kiosk is still open. Perhaps we could sit there.'

'Perhaps we could.'

'They have fairly good coffee.' He threw a few desperate scraps of food into the lake. The ducks, mostly mallards, fanned about them madly and from across the water three gulls swept like pairs of flying scissors. 'Would you like some coffee?'

'I think it may be a good idea. Thank you.'

The seats at the kiosk were under indigo blue umbrellas and had kept dry. The colour of the umbrellas reminded him of the notepaper she used. In some extraordinary way the diffusion of it in the rather dull evening air made her face seem to shrink and become plainer and thinner than ever.

While waiting for the coffee to arrive he said several times that he hoped it wouldn't rain again. She said she hoped so too. He said, several times also, that he liked feeding the ducks. It was his favourite place along here, even in winter. He was always coming here. It whiled away the time.

All the time he was dreading the moment when she would ask about the pin, which he hadn't brought with him and never would and as soon as the coffee arrived he passed the sugar to her and said in an effort to be casual:

'Where are you from?'

'I am from Austria.'

'Ah! Vienna. I have never been there.'

'I am from near Linz. Not Vienna.'

'Have you been in England long?'

'Nearly one year.'

The evening sun was actually breaking through the clouds by now, making vapour rise from the lake edge. The ducks were paddling about in a light cloud of steam and as he watched them he started to ponder on the name Vibert. It sounded rather more French than German, he thought.

'Do you pronounce Vibert to rhyme with *bear* or with *hurt*?' he said.

Perhaps it was the very clumsiness or silliness of this that made her seem suddenly ill-at-ease. She didn't answer for some seconds and he said:

'I only asked because it seemed rather like a French name.'

'Oh! yes. That is so. My father was French. His mother was named Aimée.'

Slowly sipping his coffee, he started to have fresh thoughts about the name.

'In a funny sort of way,' he said, 'I seem to have heard your name before.'

'Sometimes it is happening like that.'

'Aimée Vibert,' he started to say, 'it sort of –'

'Truly speaking my father was not really French. He came to Austria as a boy. He was brought up there. He even could hardly speak French.'

Most of the time she fixed a hopeless stare on the lake, more than half hiding her face every time she lifted the coffee cup to it with both hands. He was still too shy to watch her very closely but whenever he did so he felt the once provocative image of a dark-haired woman carrying the scent of carnations in her hair grow fainter and fainter.

After an especially long silence he once again became scared that she would ask about the pin and he said:

'What do you do?'

'I hope to be children's nurse.'

'Hope? Is it so difficult?'

'To find the right family is difficult. I myself am from a good family.'

'So naturally –'

'Naturally. After all it is not in every family that the mother gives her daughter a diamond hair-pin for a birthday –'

He felt his insides turn sick and sour at this pointed mention of the pin but even in this spasm of physical misery he managed to say:

'I thought it was your aunt gave it to you?'

'Yes: that is so. My mother gave me one and my aunt the other. They were a pair, you see.'

'I see. Would you like some more coffee?'

'I think so. Please.'

After he had fetched fresh cups of coffee from the kiosk he felt his dread about the pin increasing. At the same time he was whipped by curiosity to know what her own pin looked like and if she had brought it with her.

'No. I have not brought it this time.'

'Why not?'

'I felt I had to see what you were like first.'

He felt himself violently sweating again. At the same time a gull rode stridently across the lake, a fish in its mouth, screamingly pursued by two others diving in battle. He looked up and actually saw a pink fin, like a rosy arrowhead, sticking out of the long gull's beak before the two darting pursuers drove it away across the water.

'There's a battle for you. Do you find the birds exciting?'

'I really don't know.' Her voice sounded flat and monotonous. 'I hadn't thought about it.'

'I do. I'm always here watching them. You never know what you'll see. Like that fight, I mean.'

'You come alone?'

'Mostly.'

'Haven't you any friends?'

'Not really.'

His excruciating shyness seemed to snap a pair of clips across the lids of his eyes. He felt his eyeballs stiffen defensively as she tried to probe out yet another detail of his life:

'You live alone?'

'Oh! yes.'

And then, as he sat transfixed as a butterfly on a pin, she stirred rapidly at her coffee and said:

'Did you bring the pin with you?'

'Well –'

For a few desperate moments he resisted new agonies, finally pulled himself together and managed to frame a line or two he had rehearsed for most of the day:

'No, I didn't, actually. It's being repaired. One of the diamonds became loose and dropped out. It'll take a day or two –'

'Is it the one at the top? You know, where the bend is?'

'Yes,' he said, 'that's the one.'

'It was always coming out, she said.

He sat in the big silent trap of his own making, head down, utterly at a loss for anything to say. When after some time he looked up again he saw her completely engrossed in a dark stare across the lake. She might have been casting her mind far back to a troubled incident of some sort and it made him say:

'Is Austria nice? What is it like in Austria?'

Without any hesitation at all she said:

'In winter there are great snows.'

'Ah! yes, I suppose so.'

'Sometimes they drifted many metres up the walls of the Schloss.'

'Schloss?'

'The castle. Where I worked.'

The pronunciation of the word 'worked' was so strange that it might well have been 'walked' but he had no time to ponder on this before she said hastily:

'Where I lived I mean.'

'A big castle?'

'Austria is full of castles. There are castles everywhere.'

'I should like to go there once,' he said. 'But not in winter. I feel the cold a great deal and I don't like snow.'

'No? It is very beautiful.'

'I prefer summer. When I think of castles I think of big pine-trees and roses growing over the walls and –'

'Roses? What makes you think of roses?'

'I've no idea,' he said.

Another imponderable silence fell between them like a cloud. On the edge of the lake a quarrel feathered up between a pigeon and a gull. There was a steely smacking of wings and a string of snarls from the gull's beak. Farther out a duck stood on its head, orange feet clawing the air like the hands of a drowning swimmer.

Merely for something to say he asked:

'Is your companion from Austria too?'

'My companion?'

'Miss Winter, isn't that her name?'

'Oh! Anna. I didn't quite catch. Yes, she is from Austria too.'

'Is she older than you?'

'Oh! no. She is the same age. The same age exactly.'

Once again the conversation broke down. Shyness drew down the inevitable cloud under which she stared at the lake and in which he separated golden grains of sugar at the bottom of his cup with a coffee spoon.

A sudden squawk from a gull had the effect of starting off his mind in a complete revolution. He was abruptly conscious of a marked click! in his brain, like that of a lens in a camera being set, and it made him jerk out a single word.

'Roses,' he said.

'Please? What did you say?'

The incredible plainness of her face, darkly stained by the blue of the umbrella overhead, made the sharp turn of her head excruciatingly painful. It was now as if she too had been caught in a trap.

There was a rose, he had suddenly recalled, named Aimée Vibert. It was an old one, pure white, and his grandfather had grown it on a wall. The link connecting that wall with the *Schloss* far away on some Austrian mountainside whipped itself into a noose that tautened round his throat and he hardly heard her say:

'I didn't quite catch what you said again.'

'I was wondering if you'd like some more coffee, that's all.'

'I think I would, please.'

He again picked up the empty coffee cups and took them back to the kiosk. A woman polishing a glass behind the counter said 'Just in time, dear. Closing down in five minutes,' and filled up the two cups with milky coffee again. He paid for them, took his change, picked up the cups and started to walk back to the table, his hands trembling.

'I was just in time. They'll soon be closing.'

'Yes, it's getting late.'

For some time he had had a growing suspicion that, just as there was no pin, there was no *Schloss*, no companion, no aunt either: nothing but the plain dull face, its hopeless stare and the straight short hair where no hair-pin could ever possibly have sat. The diamond had never fallen from the crest of the pin. There was no Aimée Vibert and the romantic image of a dark-haired woman with the scent of carnations in her hair now sat away in a far corner somewhere, a ghost of a cooled imagination.

'I was wondering,' he said. He stirred his coffee with laborious, thoughtful strokes of the spoon. 'Will you be going back to Austria?'

'I don't think so. At least not for some time.'

'I see.'

'There is plenty of time for the pin if that is what you are thinking.'

'Oh! yes, it will be some time yet.'

The sudden mention of the pin after such a long interval unnerved him again. He gulped at his coffee quickly and then said:

'What made you leave Austria? I mean if you like it and it's so beautiful?'

She looked slowly across the lake, her stare darker again.

'You are interested in that?'

'I'm sorry. I didn't mean to intrude.'

She picked up her coffee spoon and balanced it on the edge of the cup. The bowl floated for a fraction of a second and then sank.

'I wanted to get away from myself. I was in a little trouble there.'

He could find nothing to say to this and laboriously sipped his coffee, not looking at her.

'A friend of mine was killed.'

'I'm sorry.'

'It's strange I should talk to you about it. When I don't wish to remember it.'

'There's no need to talk.'

'I haven't talked to anyone about it for one year.'

For the first time his clumsy deceit about the hair-pin struck him as impossibly and painfully idiotic; he felt suddenly cramped with shame.

'It was just an accident.'

'I see.'

'But it looked perhaps that I was responsible.'

Again he had nothing to say. In the last ten minutes the light across the lake had faded perceptibly and on the far side a floating pair of gulls shone like ghosts too.

'It was something that began as a joke and then –'

'A man?'

She paused for some moments and then said:

'No, a girl. We worked at the *Schloss* together.' This time there was no mistaking the word; it was worked, not walked. 'It's really a hotel.'

So he was right, he thought. She had made it all up. Like the pin –

'I was very fond of her. I did a stupid thing to make her jealous. Just a little stupid thing.'

That was all. The picture, incomplete though it was, flared up before him with a brief white brilliance and then darkened again. He got up. For a moment he didn't want to know any more. The idiotic deceit about the pin gnawed at him like a persistent rat and he drew his long fingers across his face several times as if forcing it away.

'You are going now?' she said.

'I think so. If you are ready.'

She got up too and then, without looking at her, he said: 'Before we go would you mind if I asked you something?'

'Please?'

'I suppose you know there is a rose named Aimée Vibert?'

'Yes,' she said. She had come across it in a magazine; she had done it on the spur of the moment; it was because she didn't want to use her proper name.

There was a break in her voice, not so much apologetic as an invitation for him to say something, to tell her perhaps that he understood her feelings and her motives about it all. He knew that the moment had come when he had to say he understood and to tell her too that everything about the pin was a fake. It was all false; he was a fake too. He had cheated in the hope of acquiring the experience of something romantic and all he had got was that plain dark face with its hopeless stare and now there was no hope of explaining it all. He simply said:

'My grandfather grew that rose. That's how I knew about it.'

She didn't speak. They started to walk slowly along the lake-side. In a vacuum of indecision he stared ahead, watching the street lights come on beyond the park. The yellow rays of them, like strong moonlight, struck upwards into the leaves of the street-trees, miraculously heightening the pattern of colours, shapes and veins.

'My name is really Anna Winter,' she said and the voice was so low that he hardly caught the rest: 'Now you know all about me.'

Through sudden humiliation at what she had said he made an abrupt and incredible conquest of shyness. He actually looked her in the face and said:

'Would you mind if I walked home with you?'

'I would not mind.'

They walked slowly on and once, as they stopped before crossing the road, he held her back from the passing traffic by catching at one of the impossible shoulder flaps of her mackin-tosh. She turned and looked up at him, the immensely trans-parent eyes quite still under the street lights.

He didn't speak.

'Yes?' she said. 'I thought you were going to say something.'

He was moved yet again to a sudden confession about the hair-pin and then, instead, heard himself incredibly uttering the words:

'Perhaps I could see you tomorrow.'

'If you would like it.'

'The pin won't be ready of course. These things take time.'

'Everything takes time.'

He guided her across the road, still holding the flap of the mackintosh. He had nothing much more to say. He had said for the time being all he had the courage to say but every now and then, as they walked on in silence, it seemed to him that the face beside him was plain no longer.

A Dream of Fair Women

AFTER he had taken his pills and done a stiff and dedicated three quarters of an hour on his stretching-and-exercising machine – both the pills and the machine were guaranteed to increase your height by several inches, expand your chest and make you live longer – Sydney Palmer took a deck-chair out of the tool-shed and went into the back garden to dream about women. Sydney was eighteen, short, soft-eyed and sandy-haired and looked not at all unlike a dormouse waking from the long sleep of winter.

Sometimes he dreamt about women much older than himself: healthy mature women like Mrs Fortescue, who ran the tea-trolley at the printing works where he was serving his apprenticeship. Mrs Fortescue seemed to him a sensational person. For several weeks she had exercised over him an influence that was nothing less than grand hypnosis. She was a big but beautifully proportioned woman, with light fluffy golden hair and splendid, promiscuous indigo-coloured eyes. Her body was as rich as a side of beef and she carried with her, always, the deep and searching perfume of clove carnations.

Although he had hardly ever spoken more than a dozen words to her he had managed, dreaming away in the deck-chair in the back-garden, to persuade Mrs Fortescue to leave her husband and run away with him to the South Pacific, where they had lived together for some time on a deserted atoll.

It had been a fevered, paradisiacal, tormenting affair. They had lived like Adam and Eve. Unclothed and unashamed, Mrs Fortescue had taught him things about love that were utterly sensational. It was at this time, when he was climbing a coconut palm one day, that he decided to get the stretching machine. The way Mrs Fortescue stood and gazed up at him from the foot of the palm, quite naked, her breasts so like splendid halved coconuts themselves, suddenly opened up all the delights of being taller. He was truly grateful to that palm.

Already he was sure he had put on an inch and a quarter in height. His muscles as he flexed them in front of the bathroom mirror popped in and out like knotted snakes and he felt singularly virile in every way. Unhappily Mrs Fortescue had suddenly left the printing works and the effect of these striking changes in him were lost on her.

But this no longer mattered. Today he had decided he was going to dream about someone else. This time it was Miss Sumpter, the girl who served in the fruit shop round the corner. Miss Sumpter was an aloof, brown-haired girl with prominent high breasts and lovely soft gooseberry-coloured eyes. He liked her long bare arms too and her hands that were always as white and shining as strips of new-washed celery.

She was altogether younger than Mrs Fortescue and quite different in every way. Mrs Fortescue oozed all the richness of the flesh; the South Pacific itself became voluptuous when she swam in it. But the thing that struck him most about Miss Sumpter was a kind of vestal purity. It was sort of Grecian, he told himself. Her very aloofness flowered, making her even more exciting than the bolder Mrs Fortescue.

He had never spoken more than a few dozen words to Miss Sumpter either, and then only to ask for a pound of grapes, a hand of bananas or things of that sort, but nevertheless he had decided to take her to Athens today. That was where she belonged, he thought: to Greece and the Greek Islands, the classical landscapes of long ago.

It was happily Saturday afternoon and soon, in his dream, they were on the afternoon plane. It was the champagne flight, of course – this wasn't the reckless abandoned affair that had borne naked fruit under South Sea palms – and he was determined that for Miss Sumpter, everything should be the absolute tops.

'I thought three or four days in Athens would be nice. And then we could go out to one of the islands. What about that?'

'You know so much more about these things than I do.'

'Well, it's just that Athens may be very hot. And then we'd be more alone on one of the islands.'

He held Miss Sumpter by the hand; the gooseberry-green

eyes glanced away and quivered. He looked swiftly at the high pronounced breasts perfectly shaped under her blouse of yellow silk and felt his body tingle.

'One of the islands then?'

'If that's what you want.'

He squeezed Miss Sumpter's cool celery-like fingers with rising enthusiasm; things were going splendidly.

'Of course I do.' A leading question suddenly occurred to him. 'Have you brought your swimming costume?'

'Two.'

'We'll swim all day,' he said, the words molten in his throat, 'and perhaps all night too.'

Athens itself was molten; the city and its surrounding gold-brown crust of hills quivered and sizzled under a barbarous sun. The Acropolis was a crown of melting candles.

He was glad when Miss Sumpter confessed that she couldn't sleep at night for the heat, the sound of traffic and the torment of flies. There was a little boat, he told her, that round-tripped the islands, just a sort of local bus service. They could take it tomorrow and hop off where and when the fancy took them.

Fancy took them, the following day, to an island whose waterfront seemed to have been built by the hands of children, with bricks of blue and peppermint-green and salt-white and sugar-pink. Great cochineal oleanders clothed the rocks, with cypress in black columns above them, with many vines and occasional vast mulberry trees dark with ripening fruit.

They stayed at a little hotel some way along the coast, its wooden framework locked on a precipice, fifty feet above the sea. Vermilion strings of geranium and skeins of blue morning-glory twined everywhere on walls and fences. Musing donkeys, straddled by even more musing women, climbed the hot mountain road. The sea was vaporous with great heat and the white sand of the shore, though shaded here and there by vast brooding olives, scalded the feet of Miss Sumpter and himself as they ran down to swim.

'How you know about these marvellous places I simply can't think –'

'Ah! well. Experience –'

He had in fact read all of it up in a travel magazine; he was great on travel magazines.

'Shall we swim? or shall we lie in the shade?'

In the molten core of the white afternoon the shade of a big black-limbed olive seemed a blissful dark oasis.

'Let's lie in the shade.'

They lay together on the sand, eating mulberries they had gathered on the way to the shore. The mulberries were delicious and turned Miss Sumpter's lips an urgent purple. He was glad to see that Miss Sumpter was wearing a white swim-suit. It seemed to heighten all the vestal nature of her body. He watched with mounting eagerness the rise and fall of her young breasts as she breathed and presently he started stroking the smooth bow of her shoulder.

'Are you glad we came?'

'Terribly.'

As the gooseberry-green eyes gazed up at him with their own absorbed dreaminess he kissed her full on her empurpled lips, at the same time slipping one hand into the warm crook of her armpit.

Soon they were locked together in restless torment. This, he thought, was paradise. This was greater than Mrs Fortescue. He felt twenty feet taller as his hand made gentle explorations of Miss Sumpter's body and Miss Sumpter, in return, gave out frequent sighs, low and soft in appeal, that were somewhere between modest protest and exquisite acceptance.

'Have you ever had an experience like this before?'

'Never,' she said. 'Have you?'

'Well –' He was half-tempted to tell her of Mrs Fortescue and then said: 'Not exactly. But every time I used to see you in the shop I'd go home and imagine this was how it would be.'

'You did? I didn't dream you thought about me like that –'

'Oh! yes, for ages.'

And to think, she said, that all the time she was thinking like that about him. His heart leapt as she told him this and he said:

'You mean you thought of us lying here like this? Kissing. Perhaps even – you know –'

'Lots and lots of times. Especially in bed at night.'

A flaming desire to touch her even more intimately whipped through him fiercely and he slipped a hand under the curve of her breasts. She stirred restlessly and made an uneasy appeal:

'Please. You mustn't do that. At least not here. People will see –'

'Nobody will see.'

'But not now. Not here.'

'Where then?' he said. Her body, though not so rich and mature as Mrs Fortescue's, was far more exquisite. It was as soft and delicate as a rose and he wanted to bury himself deep in the heart of it. 'Where then? When?'

'There's always a night, isn't there?' she said. 'You said we could swim at night.'

When it was night he lay entwined with Miss Sumpter on the sand. Her breasts were golden in the moonlight and warm to his lips as he kissed them. The sea was glassy and calm. Farther down the bay, in the hot windless night, the lights of the little town quivered like so many fireflies.

He was about to come to the supreme moment of his companionship with Miss Sumpter when she suddenly gave a quick mischievous laugh and wriggled out of his arms and started to run for the sea. Even that was a pretty wonderful moment, he thought – to see that white figure, half-naked, lightly dancing into the thin phosphorescent line of little breaking waves.

He laughed too and ran after her. Nowhere were the waves more than an inch or two in height and they broke like a lapping of warm milk on his feet. In breathless excitement he saw Miss Sumpter swimming fast out to sea and suddenly something made him shout:

'Watch out! There are sharks!'

She gave a cry as she heard this and turned at once and came swimming swiftly back.

'You didn't mean that. You were just trying to frighten me.'

'No, no, no.' He was quite serious. There were indeed sharks; he had read about them too in an article somewhere. 'A man lost a leg only last year over in Corfu. In full view of people promenading –'

'Oh! my goodness.'

Miss Sumpter confessed to feeling a little sick. It was almost as if he had saved her life, she said.

At this he felt ten feet tall again and recklessly clasped Miss Sumpter in his arms, as if in splendid protection, thrusting his chest strongly against her bosom. To his delight she accepted this demonstration of male protectiveness with a great sigh, looking at him beseechingly with the soft gooseberry-green eyes. She was so thankful, she said. His concern for her safety had opened her eyes to the fact that he didn't merely covet her for her body's sake and all the complex desires and thrills that went with it. It wasn't merely passion driving him on. He really loved her actual existence. He was really frightened she might be taken away.

'Oh! you're so nice,' she said. She looked with admiration at his figure, god-like in the moonlight. 'So wonderful.'

He laughed and kissed her mouth, salty and wet from the sea. She looked such a glorious creature standing there half-naked in the moonlight, hair and face and shoulders still dripping with water, that he actually felt pretty god-like. By heaven, he was in great shape, he told himself. The stretching machine had done wonders. He could feel manhood pulsating through him like a brave hammer. The gleam of moonlight on his face might have been striking down on the brass of some tall and splendid helmet.

'Let's swim out together,' Miss Sumpter said. 'I shan't mind about the sharks if you swim with me.'

'No,' he said. 'Let's lie on the beach. Let's just let the sea break over us. All night long.'

In that brilliant and somehow solemn moonlight they were god and goddess lying side by side. Their bodies might have been made of gold and when at last another supreme moment arrived and Miss Sumpter leaned over to kiss him the young breast that touched his face was a golden apple beaded all over with the pearls of a divine and ancient sea.

He opened his eyes and suddenly leapt up out of the deck-chair, all sweat, unable to bear it any longer. So real were the rays of Grecian moonlight, Miss Sumpter's body and the phosphorescence of the sea that when he stared about him it was the back-garden that swayed, unreal in the afternoon sun.

There was nothing for it, he told himself; he had to go round to the fruit shop. He had somehow to see Miss Sumpter, perhaps even talk to her, before the brilliant reality of the dream faded away. It was inconceivable that that realistic episode could have failed to get through to her.

Perhaps, he asked himself as he half-ran into the house, he ought to do another ten minutes on the stretching-machine before he went? and then decided against it. It was clearly imperative to see her while the potency of the dream was so brilliant and so powerful.

He paused to look at himself in the bathroom mirror, brushing his sweaty hair. He looked uncommonly pale and hot after all the exertions of making love with Miss Sumpter and his eyes had in them a moist and dilated glow. Several times he expanded his chest and tautened the muscles of his arms and once, just before departing for the shop, he stood immovably at attention, drawing up his figure to its full height.

The fruit shop was crowded with customers. Miss Sumpter, lost in the heart of the crowd, was serving several pounds of onions to an elderly lady wearing a purple hat. The rustle of onion skins fell on his ears like the tormenting echo of many little waves breaking on a distant shore.

'No hurry,' he said several times to other assistants. The lady in the purple hat was buying peas now, fussily cracking open a pod or two in order to test their tenderness. 'No hurry. Thank you, I'll wait.'

'Yes? What for you, please?'

It was the aloof, vestal Miss Sumpter, free at last. He stood impotently before her, trying desperately to feel god-like again, hardly able to look at her. Her face, with its lovely gooseberry-green eyes, swam mistily in a frame of bananas and flowers, apples and cucumbers, apricots and onions. As these dissolved even more mistily into a background of Grecian waves gently lapping under a golden moon Miss Sumpter said, rather tartly:

'Well? We're awfully busy.'

His whole body made a stammering effort at control and in the most ungod-like of voices he said:

'A pound of apples, please.'

'Jonathans? Cox's? Cookers?'

'Cox's.'

It was the shortest word of the three but it seemed to take a whole aeon of time to pronounce it.

'Something else?'

'Bananas.'

'How many would you like?'

'Two pounds, please.'

She was immensely aloof, dreadfully distant. He was unable even to look at her hands, let alone the breast that had touched his face like a golden apple. She had become infinitely more than a stranger: she simply didn't belong to his world.

'Anything more?'

'Well, I must just think.'

He tried to think. His mind hovered like a cowering bat in a suspense of cavernous gloom.

'Any celery today?'

'Not today. Hasn't started to come in. Hasn't had a frost on it yet.'

If there had been no frost on the celery there was a searing and darkening frost on the voice of Miss Sumpter. It seemed to cut down his stature by several inches. He stared helplessly this way and that and then said at last:

'I think that'll be all, then, thank you.'

'Three and nine. Pay at the desk.'

That final impersonal note wiped every remaining image of the dream from his mind. He wavered briefly on the point of departure and then in a courageously desperate moment decided there was something else he wanted to ask for.

'Do you happen to have mulberries at all?'

She would surely, he thought, remember the mulberries.

'Do we have what?'

'Mulberries. You know –'

'Oh! mulberries. Yes. Three and six a tin.'

'You don't have fresh ones?'

'Didn't know they ever came fresh.' She actually laughed, cutting him deeply, and turned away.

'Yes, madam? Watercress?'

Cooled and impotent, he went home to the back-garden and the deck-chair. He knew he never wanted to dream of Miss Sumpter again. She had crushed the dream under her feet like the shell of a snail. Her cold and impersonal nature wrapped him about like a fog. He started slowly to peel a banana and then shut his eyes in a grim and calculated effort to shut her image out.

Presently he was dreaming instead of a girl named Shirley Chalmers, a typist, who worked in the office at the printing works. She, like Miss Sumpter and Mrs Fortescue, was rather taller than himself but she had, he was sure, both a nicer and more sympathetic nature. Her figure was very beautiful and her hair, which she wore rather long, was an exotic deep bluish-black, with a clear shine on it like that of ripe elderberries in September.

He had a strange idea too that Miss Chalmers wore black underwear; he had once caught a brief glimpse of shadowy lace under the hem of her skirt as she ran upstairs, her legs meltingly seductive. For some reason he thought that girls who wore black underwear were exceptionally passionate. Warm, friendly blood, he was sure, flowed through Miss Chalmers' veins. She was also, he felt certain, a person of great understanding. You could tell that by the fine depth of stillness in her eyes.

She was just the sort of girl, he now decided, to take to Morocco. Ah! the bougainvilleas and the palms, the markets and the *Kasbah*, the mystery, the heat and the mountains – what a wonderful thing it would be to have a companion like Miss Chalmers there, the exotic, passionate, understanding Miss Chalmers.

He needed a companion like Miss Chalmers. He needed her very, very much.

A Nice Friendly Atmosphere

A FINE male blackbird was singing throatily, with two cuckoos calling in the near gold-green distances of oak and chestnut and a woodpecker laughing somewhere beyond them, almost in mockery, as Mr and Mrs Barclay sat down to lunch on the first Sunday in May.

'What is this?' Mr Barclay said and proceeded to prod the joint of meat in front of him with the wrong end of the gravy spoon.

It was the leg of boar, in the Pyrenees style, *Pierria di Jabali a la Pirenaica*, Mrs Barclay explained, that they had in Spain last year. The only difference was that she had had to do it with leg of mutton. Nor had it been possible to get the globe artichokes the dish called for so early in May and she had had to do the best she could with swede turnips, though she thought that with lavish use of the *sauce espagnole* you would hardly notice the change.

'The possibility of life on Uranus?' Mr Barclay said. The gravy spoon, poised in air, seemed to be held ready for the act of carving. 'No, I don't think so.'

This was Mr Barclay's answer to a question, put quite some time before, by his elder daughter Philippa, who was twelve and wore her coarse fair hair long and loose, in the style of Alice in Wonderland.

'Yes, but do we know?' she said. 'Is it a fact, I mean? Are we certain?'

Mr Barclay, now vaguely prodding the meat about as if searching for some favourable point at which to make an incision, confessed that he supposed they were not. The great distance of the planet precluded any certainty.

'Yes, but what do we mean by life? That's what I want to know.'

The youngest of the Barclay children, Henry, put his question in a severe inquisitorial treble. He was seven. He was wearing a thick dark blue polo-neck sweater, home-knitted and three sizes too big for him. His brown-rimmed spectacles were large and thick and gave him the look of an inquiring deep-sea diver who had just surfaced from under the table.

'There's no point in being vague,' he said.

'Astronomically speaking,' Michaela said – she, the middle one of the Barclay children, wore her stiffish onion-brown hair in a plain round bob that might have been idly trimmed up with the aid of a colander some weeks before – 'I suppose there is no such thing as uncertainty.'

'Quite. What did Pope say?' Philippa said. ' "Whatever is, is right" ?'

'Exactly,' Henry said. 'Absolutely.'

Mr Barclay now actually exchanged the gravy spoon for the carving fork and gave the *Pierria di Jabali a la Pirenaica* a sharp poke with it. A protesting squeak, like that from a tight leather sole, came out of it, but Mr Barclay took no notice at all, merely declaring instead that Michaela was quite correct. Science knew no uncertainty.

'Those blasted bull-finches are playing hell with the cherry-buds again!' Henry suddenly shouted, shaking a dirty fist. 'I'll murder the lot!' The greedy bastards!'

Mrs Barclay, who was wearing a dark brown hairy sweater, also home-knitted, and who would have been pretty in a mole-like way if only she had used lipstick and left her light brown hair to grow naturally instead of pinching it into a stringy Victorian bun that hung well down her neck, started spooning mashed potatoes and brussels sprouts on to the plates that Mr Barclay had so far left empty. The potatoes, steaming ever so slightly, had a grey, cement-like look about them and the brussels sprouts the appearance of old chestnuts parboiled in soot water.

Mr Barclay, after solemnly reminding Henry that everything had to live and that in the very nature of things bull-finches couldn't differentiate between good and evil, again stuck the carving fork into the mutton. Nature was neither moral nor immoral, he said and picked up a butter knife in preparation, at last, to start carving the meat.

'Help yourselves to the *sauce espagnole*,' Mrs Barclay said to the children, as if in veiled warning that the meat might be some time in reaching them yet.

Mr Barclay, who was thirty-two, prematurely bald and rather podgy, was wearing a shirt of Italian-red flannel, expansive blue shorts, horn-rimmed spectacles and a pair of Spanish slippers made of rice-straw. He had somehow managed to get himself a government grant to attend classes at Art School four times a week. He painted rather well on silks. It was a bit of a struggle, even with a cottage in the country, to get through.

'Telephone!' Henry said and sprang up from the table as if to answer the ringing of the bell.

'I'll go,' Mr Barclay said.

In the sudden absence of Mr Barclay his wife seized the opportunity to start carving the *Pierria di Jabali a la Pirenaica*, mutton style. She had been dreadfully suspicious for some time that all was not quite well with it. Perhaps she had marinated the meat too long; or perhaps not long enough. The principal thing she understood about cooking was that, as in science, you applied heat to things and certain changes took place. In due course, in a miraculous way, objects became fried, boiled, baked, steamed or casseroled. If the taste in most cases was very much the same this seemed to make little difference, at least to the children, who didn't know any difference anyway and were always as ravenous as vultures.

'Who was it for?' she said. In the absence of Mr Barclay, now back at the table, she had succeeded in stabbing off several stumpy cuts of meat and serving them out to the children. The mutton, which had been cooking for some four hours, still seemed decidedly gristly. Perhaps, she thought, she ought to have cooked it longer?

'Nobody,' Mr Barclay said. 'The line was dead.'

Mr Barclay stared at the plateful of meat, grey potatoes, brussels sprouts and compressed turnips, now generously covered with *sauce espagnole*, which Mrs Barclay had set before him. He was unable to distinguish between one object and another or to detect that the food was almost cold. He attacked it instead with a shovelling vigour and relish, head close over the plate, only pausing once to say:

'It doesn't taste awfully like boar, does it? You think so?'

'You must pretend it's boar,' Philippa said. 'Taste is illusory. Relative, I mean. It's merely a question of –'

'Telephone again!' Henry said and again jumped up as if to answer the bell, only to be restrained this time by Mrs Barclay, who said:

'I'll go this time. I don't think it is the telephone after all. I've a feeling it's the front door bell.'

As she left the room Henry stared hard through the open casement window at the garden, his jaws grinding moodily on a sinewy lump of *Pierria di Jabali a la Pirenaica*. This gave him a certain air of savage preoccupation as he watched a pair of bull-finches stripping to shreds, on the far side of the lawn, in a gay combination of mischief and hunger, the pink buds of a late flowering cherry-tree.

'I hate bloody bull-finches,' he said. 'I absolutely and positively hate the blasted things.'

'That's a great mistake,' Mr Barclay said. 'I've told you before – the application of human emotions to the complex structure necessary to preserve the balance of nature only leads to a falsity of attitude about life. And above all sentimentality.'

'Is that the same as the pathetic fallacy?' Michaela said.

'Not quite,' Mr Barclay said, 'but there are certain features common to –'

He paused, suddenly aware that Mrs Barclay had come back into the room. She had in fact stopped just inside the doorway, where she was anxiously and dryly rubbing her hands together.

'There's a man here,' she whispered, 'who says you invited him to Sunday lunch.'

'Never. Impossible. We're half way through it anyway.'

'He seems awfully positive about it.'

'He can't be. Ask him what his name is.'

'I did and –'

'It's Floater, Mr Barclay!' a voice called with muscular familiarity like a clarion from the passage outside. 'It's me, Mr Barclay. Floater.'

'Good grief!' Mr Barclay said. 'I could have sworn it was next Sunday.'

'Who is Floater?' Mrs Barclay said.

'Take it calmly,' Mr Barclay said. 'He's from Art School. He's had a marvellously interesting life. He's been everywhere.'

'Well, since he's arrived here too I'd better put the meat back into the oven. This sort of dish is never so good if it gets cold.'

While Mrs Barclay hastily took away the *Pierria di Jabali a la Pirenaica*, now less than lukewarm, Mr Barclay rushed forward towards the passage with extravagant greeting, saying:

'Floater, my dear fellow, Floater. We thought you were never coming. We'd given you up.'

'Eh? You told me –'

'Sit down. Here, next to me. I fear we've started, but only just. Philippa, Henry, Michaela – this is Floater Pearson. I'll get some beer.'

Floater Pearson gave a large friendly grin and sat down at table.

'Morning all,' he said.

'Strictly speaking it's afternoon,' Michaela said. 'Good afternoon.'

'I see,' Floater said. 'It's like that, is it?'

'Well, it's either afternoon or it's not, isn't it?' Philippa said. 'It can't be both at the same time.'

Floater Pearson, looking rather wistfully about the table, said it wasn't afternoon with him, not until he'd had his dinner; and he hadn't had it yet.

'That's a mere arbitrary distinction,' Michaela said.

'Time is time,' Henry said. 'You can't change it. Don't be so artificial.'

Floater Pearson opened his mouth sharply and then, utterly at a loss, shut it again, so that the upper plate of his false teeth gave a bony snap. He seemed slightly affronted, even hurt.

'Blimey, I –'

Floater started to protest and then, with a gasp, gave up. He was rather tall, very broad in the shoulders, which were padded out, and narrow at the waist, where his trousers were held up by a thong of plaited leather by a magenta and chromium buckle shaped like a mermaid. His suit was a bright plum colour. His shirt, a pure canary, had an accompanying white tie patterned with prominent blue figures, a climbing galaxy of naked buxom girls.

'I'm seven,' Henry said. 'How old are you?'

Floater scratched his intensely black head of hair and said he was a year younger than Mr Barclay. He knew because they'd compared notes the other day.

'That makes you thirty-one,' Henry said. 'And where did you come from?'

'Oh! I live at Fordstone,' Mr Pearson said. 'Near the Art School.'

'I didn't mean like that,' Henry said. 'I meant in the first place. I came from a cell. You did too, I expect.'

Floater Pearson suddenly laughed with singing clarity, showing three gold teeth in his broad and rather handsome mouth.

'Could be,' he said. 'Could be.'

'What exactly do you take at Art School?' Philippa said.

Floater laughed again, rather more warily this time.

'Mostly what I can catch,' he said.

During this conversation he had become more and more fascinated by what the children had on their plates. It puzzled him considerably. There was nothing recognizable at all in the mess of brown and white and orange lumps except perhaps the potato. As if sensing his doubts Henry said:

'This is boar. We had it in Spain last year.'

'Boar?'

'A male pig. Only wild of course. It's mutton really.'

'Good Gawd,' Floater said.

Here Michaela interposed to say that what Philippa had really been asking was whether Mr Pearson painted or sculpted or what? Floater scratched his head again, in what was evidently a favourite gesture of his and was just beginning to explain that as a matter of fact he wasn't exactly at Art School any longer when Mr Barclay came back into the room with a big glass jug of beer and two glasses.

'Well, here's the beer,' he said. 'The food won't be a minute.'

A moment later, as Mr Barclay started to pour the beer out,

Henry suddenly got up and threw his dinner out of the open window, plate and all. Mr Barclay took no notice whatever of this; nor did Philippa and Michaela who went on eating with a voracity almost enraptured.

'What's he gone and done that for?' Floater said.

'He obviously doesn't like it,' Michaela said. 'Unless you can think of another explanation.'

Floater couldn't think of any explanation at all; he sat mute. At this moment Henry returned to the table with a large orange which he began to peel by savagely biting lumps off it with his front teeth. Several of these lumps he threw straight up into the air without bothering to look where they fell. One of them in fact fell on to Mr Barclay's plate, the contents of which had now congealed quite solid, but he took no notice of that either.

'Well, here's to the wallop,' Mr Barclay said. This sudden and unexpected concession to politeness so startled Floater Pearson that he actually stopped dead in the act of lifting his glass. It was then that he thought he detected something very peculiar about the beer.

It was a sort of strange muddy yellow, he noticed. It looked as if it might have been made with a curious type of floor polish. A few dark objects, rather like dismembered tadpoles, were slowly floating up to the surface of it.

Before he could make up his mind to take a sample drink of it Mrs Barclay was back with the food, which was now steaming prodigiously. This was because Mrs Barclay had decided that her best course was to cut up the remainder of the lamb, sub-merge it in *sauce espagnole* and fry it all up rapidly with a bit more pepper.

Floater, suddenly depressed and feeling appetite leaving him at every breath, merely stared hard at the beer. Mrs Barclay for some reason seemed to take this as a sign of anticipatory relish and said with enthusiasm:

'Ah! yes, Floater, you must tell us what you think of our beer.'

'Your beer?'

At this moment Henry got down from table and kicked the

entire orange, football fashion, into the air. It fell perilously near to the *Pierria di Jabali a la Pirenaica* which Mrs Barclay was now serving to Floater Pearson without arousing any comment from anyone except Floater himself, who said:

'Here, blimey, watch it, mate. Turn it up.'

'It's dandelion,' Mrs Barclay said. 'It was fresh-made last week. We make it ourselves.'

Floater lowered his face to the beer. There was a very ropey smell about it, he suddenly decided. It was sort of yeasty.

By this time Mr Barclay was shovelling food into his mouth again, washing it down with positive gasps, rather than gulps, of beer.

'It has a certain tang about it, don't you think?' he said. 'You can taste the earth in it, I feel.'

That was a fact, Floater thought. That was how it tasted: a bit of the yeast and a bit of the earth. He longed deeply for a pint of mild-and-bitter. With apprehension he started to cut at the wild boar, mutton style, with his knife and fork, at the same time glancing out of the corner of his eye to see how Mr Barclay did it.

Mr Barclay, he decided, was a shocking untidy eater. With the gravy spoon in his left hand and a fork in the other he used both implements as shovels. The children were much better. With them the knife and the fork went into the mouth, as Floater knew they should, alternately.

'We make one with herbs too,' Mrs Barclay said. 'Jack-by-the-hedgeside, sorrel, thyme, wild mint – Oh! about a dozen of them. It has a fresher, more aromatic flavour than this. It's from a very old local recipe.'

'I prefer the dandelion,' Mr Barclay said. 'It has much more nose. It has that tang.'

Henry, it seemed, preferred it too. He came boldly up, took a sample of beer from Floater Pearson's glass and spat it on the floor.

'What course are you taking at Art School, Mr Pearson?' Mrs Barclay said.

'Blasted bull-finches!' Henry shouted. 'I'll murder you!'

Some of Floater Pearson's sense of humour had, by this time, deserted him. He slowly finished masticating a mouthful of mutton, washed it away with a sip of beer and said:

'Well, as a matter of fact, I was doing the boilers.'

'You mean you're not any longer?' Philippa said. 'Then why don't you say so?'

'He is what is nowadays politely called redundant,' Mr Barclay said. He spoke acidly, openly picking his teeth with a finger nail. 'In other words, he's had the sack. In my view damned unjustly.'

By this time Henry had wandered into the garden, where he was throwing stones at bull-finches. From somewhere came the startling crash of broken glass.

'He's the victim of social ostracism. Or in this case official ostracism.'

'You're damn right,' Floater said.

'You don't mind my wife knowing this, do you, Floater?' Mr Barclay said. 'As a matter of fact, Floater has done time.'

'Oh! I am sorry,' Mrs Barclay said.

'Not my fault,' Floater said. 'I never had nothing to do with it.'

'This was discovered, you understand,' Mr Barclay said, 'after eight months, by some busybody of a clerk. Eight months Floater worked at the boilers – admirably, to universal satisfaction.'

'What did you do to get imprisonment?' Michaela said. 'I'm absolutely fascinated.'

'Well, two pals of mine done a warehouse and I was supposed to be there.'

'And you weren't?' Philippa said.

'Well, I were and I weren't, see? Nothing would have happened if it hadn't been for a courting couple going by. They had to peep.'

'But that's anti-social,' Michaela said. 'They wouldn't like it if people peeped at them.'

'That's right. I was just minding my own business.'

'One debt has been paid,' Mr Barclay said, 'but now another

must be extracted. Society, the busybodies, must have another pound of flesh. I call that grossly unfair.'

'Bloody unfair,' Michaela said.

'This sort of thing,' Floater suddenly said, with an entirely new turn of righteous vehemence, 'would never happen if people would take and mind their own bleeding business.'

'It's a gossip-bed,' Philippa said, 'that Art School.'

'No, I mean the other,' Floater said. 'I had a very nice career in front of me.'

Mrs Barclay, after mopping up the last of the *Pierria di Jabali* with a hunk of bread, remarked that if you looked at it rationally, that is in a purely objective fashion, there was no such thing as right and wrong.

'After all, we would all steal a loaf of bread or a joint of meat,' she said, 'if we were hungry.'

Floater, laughing singingly again, agreed with extraordinary alacrity, delighted to find that there were people of his own way of thinking in the world.

'I never done no wrong,' he said. 'The wrong people just happened to be around, that's all.'

'What disturbs me –'

'Mind if I have a cheroot?' Floater said. He didn't usually smoke in the middle of meals but it was the only thing he could think of to take away the haunting taste of the meat and the *sauce espagnole*, which he had now managed to finish, and the dandelion beer.

'By all means,' Mrs Barclay said. 'By all means.'

'Anybody for a cheroot?' Floater said. 'Mrs Barclay?'

Mrs Barclay declined the cheroot and started to clear away the dishes.

'I'll take one,' Mr Barclay said.

'And I too,' Michaela said.

As Floater offered his cheroot case, a silver one with what seemed to be an edging of gold, Mr Barclay, with his artistic sense at once alert, seized upon it with admiration.

'That's a beautiful thing. What a nice coat-of-arms too.'

'Always been rather fond of it,' Floater said. 'Picked it up on the off-chance a long time ago.'

'Cheroots smell awfully good.'

'Nice sample,' Floater confessed with a certain ample pride. 'Makes some of 'em look pretty ropey. I like the best.'

'I'm rather afraid I can't run to them myself.'

'No?' Floater said. 'No? That's bad. Have a packet, Mr Barclay. I got quite a little stock at home.'

After again waving the silver-and-gold case and a packet of cheroots in several directions, as if to indicate limitless gener-osity, he watched with silent satisfaction as Michaela lighted her cheroot. She did so with a certain expert, adult care.

Some moments later Mrs Barclay returned from the kitchen with a small brick of whitish material, garnished with what seemed to be caraway seeds, reposing on a piece of muslin in a saucer.

'Cheese?' she asked. 'It's our own making. Or potato cake? That's another Spanish dish we're all rather partial to.'

'I want potato cake!' Henry suddenly screamed, his entrance from the garden preceded by a stupendous metallic bang, rather as if a bucket had been thrown at a wall.

Mrs Barclay was about to cut the potato cake, which had something of the appearance of a lump of rough pumice stone, when Henry advanced on her, picked up the cake and took it away. Sitting with it at the end of the table he locked a pair of broodily defensive arms about it and, as with the orange, started to gnaw lumps off the edges of it, rabbit-fashion, with his front teeth.

'I was really going to serve *Little Pigs of Heaven* today,' Mrs Barclay said, 'but—'

Good Gawd, Floater thought. Wild boar for first and now little pigs for afters. What next? He longed deeply again for a straight pint of mild-and-bitter and thought also, with incon-gruous relish, of something nice and sweet, like a good rice pudding.

'It's all sugar and eggs and chocolate sauce,' Michaela said. She puffed cheroot smoke across the table in an obliterating cloud. 'Do you know Spain?'

Floater had to confess that he didn't. Spain was out of his world. No mention having been made of the fact that Henry had apparently taken the potato cake for keeps, Floater now stared moodily at the home-made cheese, watching Mrs Barclay cutting it into small parsimonious slices. He was a bit shocked, he told himself, about Henry. It was a bit near the knuckle to take things like that. And at your ma's table too.

Mr Barclay now poured out more dandelion beer and Philippa, tucking her chin with almost accusatory earnestness into her cupped hands, said:

'Were you awfully repressed as a child?'

Floater, assuming with a typical singing laugh such as he hadn't given for some time that this meant him, said no, he didn't think so, not all that much. He was out on the spree most of the time.

'Were you beaten, I mean, an awful lot?'

'Like bleedin' hell,' Floater said. 'The old man used to belt the old woman and then she used to ruddy well take it out on me, the old bitch.' Floater blew cheroot smoke with a certain regal air, plushily off-hand, not only as if he were perhaps proud of these recollections but as if also with intention of drawing attention to an emerald ring on his right third finger and a pair of gold-and-pearl cuff-links in his canary yellow shirt sleeves.

This air of opulence was suddenly intensified as he picked up a butter knife and with it speared a piece of cheese.

'You're wearing a ring,' Mrs Barclay said. 'I really hadn't noticed it before.'

'Keepsake,' Floater said. He turned and looked Mrs Barclay full in the face, for the first time. His dark eyes had a deeply scrutinous air about them, almost luxurious in feeling, and she felt herself slipping into a state of light hypnosis as he said:

'I see you don't wear no jewellery, Mrs Barclay. You ought to, really. Would suit you.'

Mrs Barclay, with a certain coolness, deliberately withdrew into herself. She found jewellery a social vulgarity; it was like having too much money or being too successful; it really wasn't nice.

'Oh! no, I don't think so. Jewellery really isn't for me.'

'Oh! I thought you liked it sort of. You just admired my ring.'

'Well, it's rather like make-up. You can tolerate it in others while not using it yourself.'

Mr Barclay, dozy by this time, swigged at dandelion beer and then spread his elbows broadly over the table and munched pieces of home-made cheese, putting them into his mouth with his fingers.

'You still have a few pieces your mother left you, though,' he said.

'Yes,' Mrs Barclay said. 'That was why I noticed the ring. It's awfully like one of hers.'

'Oh?' Floater said. 'It is?'

'I did think at one time of saving them for the girls, but –'

'Oh! no thanks,' Michaela said. 'That primitive sex display stuff –'

As she spoke Henry hurled a large lump of potato cake as big as a croquet ball at the casement window, where it landed with a loud bang, at the same time yelling 'Cheese!' Mr Barclay dutifully passed what remained of it to him and Floater said:

'Like to have a look at that piece some time, Mrs Barclay, if I might.'

'Fetch it down,' Mr Barclay said. 'Let Floater have a look at it.'

While Mrs Barclay had gone upstairs Mr Barclay felt it opportune to ask Floater how the prospect of another job was going. Not all that well, Floater told him. It wasn't easy. The word had got round. 'I'll have to move to another districk,' he said and the words were almost sad.

'Where to?' Mr Barclay said.

'No idea yet,' Floater said. 'And if I did I wouldn't say.'

'You could tell me. You can trust me.'

That was the great thing, he thought. To impart trust. To create an atmosphere of solid, mutual reliance.

'Granted, Mr Barclay. All the same I'm keeping mum to one and all. I'm sliding out. I got to have a clean slate and it's the only way.'

'I sympathize,' Mr Barclay said. 'God, I feel bloody angry about it.'

'You do?'

'I feel angry and ashamed!' Mr Barclay said. 'Yes: I even feel ashamed!'

When Mrs Barclay at last came back with the ring, a largish one with a diamond and emerald setting, Floater purred over it as over the egg of a rare and exquisite bird.

'This 'ere's a beaut,' he said. 'Your old lady gave you this?'

'She belonged to the age that set a lot of store on these things. The old establishment. It isn't surprising it's cracked up now.'

'My God, not,' Michaela said. 'All that title muck –'

'Blah!' Philippa said. 'Blah!'

Floater now eyed the ring with a fervour so nearly amounting to reverence that he took several deepish swigs at the dandelion beer without really being aware of it.

'Want to sell it?'

'I hadn't thought of it.'

'Pay for a good many holidays in Spain.'

Mr Barclay sat upright in sharp alarm, his voice giving several unusually high croaks of inquiry.

'*Several* holidays in Spain. *Several*?'

'Of course I don't know what it costs there –'

'Oh! it's cheap,' Mrs Barclay said. 'That's the beautiful thing about it. It's cheap.'

'But *several* holidays? *Several*? How much do you think –'

'Oh! this little piece is worth about four hundred nicker – perhaps more –'

'Nicker?' Mrs Barclay said.

'Quid,' Floater said, 'pounds.'

'Good God Almighty,' Mr Barclay said, 'we could take one of these villas on the *Costa de Sol* – weeks of it, months, my God – Floater, how on earth do you come to know about these things?'

'It used to be my trade,' Floater said. His voice was ever so slightly pained; it might have been that he felt professionally slighted. 'I was in the trade.'

'My God, that would solve everything,' Mr Barclay said. 'July August, September. October even – I'd say we ought to sell.'

'Why keep this ostentatious muck?' Michaela said. 'You might as well have a lump of Uranus.'

'Quite so,' Mrs Barclay said. 'All right, I'll sell it. I don't know why I didn't before.'

'Like me to put you in touch with a good man?' Floater said. The words were skinned off the mouth with a suavity as cool and soft as a grape. 'Hatton Garden. He'll give you the tops.'

'Well, that's nice –'

Suddenly Floater, rather as if granting a favour, displayed his own ring again.

'Did a little repair job on this for me not long ago. Take a deck at that little stone there – the emerald. Come loose. He put it back again. Offered me two hundred and fifty for the ring but I said no, it was keepsake: I said no.'

'How shall we get it there?' Mrs Barclay said.

'Post,' Floater said. 'Registered. Unless you – I'll give you the address.'

'Unless what were you saying?'

'I'm going up there tomorrow,' Floater said. 'I'll be seeing this bloke. His name's Rothman. Of course that's if you trust me –'

'Trust you, man? Of course we trust you,' Mr Barclay said. 'Trust is the essence of the whole affair. As long as the Art School trusted you all was well. The moment trust was withdrawn the whole fabric crumbled.'

'Logic,' Michaela said. 'Exactly.'

'My husband is quite right,' Mrs Barclay said. 'Of course we trust you. Implicitly.'

'Well, as I say. I got to go up there on the off-chance of a job and if I can do you a good turn –'

'All the luck in the world for the job,' Mr Barclay said. 'Don't forget the reference I gave you –'

'Not likely,' Floater said. 'He always pays cash, this bloke. No trouble at all. I expect I'll be back on the six o'clock –'

'I somehow feel it's a good omen for us both,' Mr Barclay said. 'I do believe it's a good omen.'

'More cheese!' Henry started shouting and promptly threw another piece of potato cake at the window.

'Another cheroot, anybody?' Floater said and expansively waved the gold-and-silver case this way and that.

'I think I will,' Mr Barclay said, his voice thick now with dandelion beer. 'You've got good taste in that direction, I must say, Floater. Good taste.'

'I always try to have good taste, Mr Barclay,' Floater said. 'I think it goes a long way.'

'Beyond question it does,' Mrs Barclay said.

'I'll give you a receipt for the ring,' Floater said. 'Just to make it all fair and square.'

'Oh! no, no,' Mr Barclay said. 'We wouldn't dream of it. No, no, no.'

'No?' Floater said. 'Up to you.'

With a certain air of hesitation underlined by a sort of dreamy sadness he looked fondly at the ring and then gazed for some moments out of the window, remarking with almost tearful politeness what a lovely day it had been: real grand. All the ghastly accumulated recollections of lunch, of wild-boar, mutton style, *sauce espagnole*, dandelion beer, home-made cheese and potato cake were well behind him now. He wasn't even bothered by that little crook Henry any more: the little bastard, no more manners than a stray tom-cat snitching butter. Floater's Ma would have belted merry hell out of him for manners like that, no two ways about it.

'Very kind of you to have me, Mr Barclay,' he said. 'I appreciate it. It's a nice friendly atmosphere here. Real nice and friendly. You feel free.'

'Free, do you hear?' Mr Barclay said with immense enthusiasm. 'Free? Splendid.' He resisted an impulse to clap Floater firmly on the back and merely put his hand on his shoulder instead. 'Absolutely splendid – if only those busybodies at the school – Oh! well, ignore them, Floater. Forget them. We trust you, and it's trust that matters. It's the mutual confidence that tells.'

Floater, with a beaming grin, said not half it wasn't and a moment later was shaking hands with strenuous warmth all round. He'd certainly come again, he told them, in answer to a trilling invitation from Mrs Barclay. He'd like to. In fact with any luck at all he'd be dropping in tomorrow.

'Tomorrow indeed!' Mr Barclay said. 'Splendid. We shall look forward to that.'

'Me too!' Floater said and gave a last flashing, disarming wave of his hand. 'I don't half like this nice friendly atmosphere.'

When the plum-coloured suit, the canary shirt and the white tie with its galaxy of naked girls had finally disappeared, Mr Barclay went back into the dining-room to finish his beer and help Mrs Barclay with the dishes.

'I like him,' she said. 'I really like him.'

'Of course,' Mr Barclay said. 'He's a good fellow. The right material's there. You feel it. Once prejudice is ignored and mutual trust established –'

'I meant to ask him if he liked Wagner,' Philippa said. 'He looked sort of Wagnerish to me.'

'Oh! no,' Michaela said. 'Wagner is sinister.'

'I didn't mean in that sort of way. I meant he looked sort of operatic –'

'My God, three months in Spain,' Mr Barclay said. 'Let's all go into the garden and smell the air.'

'I liked what he said about feeling free here,' Mrs Barclay said. 'About the nice friendly atmosphere.'

Mr Barclay said he did too. He followed Mrs Barclay and the children into the garden. Over against the cherry tree Henry was still throwing stones at invisible bull-finches, yelling:

'I'll murder you! I'll whack your brains out, you little bastards! – I'll murder every one of you!'

Mr and Mrs Barclay, almost as if pleased with what they heard, smiled at each other.

'I knew there was something – isn't there a ring round Uranus?' Mrs Barclay said. 'That was what I meant about the omen.'

'Saturn,' Michaela said.

'I knew it was one or other,' Mrs Barclay said.

Over by the cherry tree Henry started yelling murder again and Philippa called:

'It's jackdaws you should kill. They're the ones that steal.'

'That's it,' Michaela said. 'Let's all go and kill jackdaws.'

'You can make jackdaws talk too if you cut their tongues.'

'All right, let's cut their tongues,' Henry said. 'I've got an old razor blade. Come on, let's cut their tongues with an old razor blade.'

'Well, let's kill something first,' Philippa said and started running ferociously across the lawn, followed by Michaela and Henry, whooping blood-thirstily. 'I'm bored.'

As if in echo a cuckoo called in the near distances and somewhere farther away a solitary woodpecker laughed on hollow, almost idiotic notes, seeming to mock at it, as in fact it had done for most of the day.

The Lotus Land

THE road ran black and straight and shining between tall plantations of coconut palms, through which was sometimes visible, a few hundred yards away, the black sand of the shore. Beyond that, a mile or more out to sea, great jagged white waves burst on the coral reef, tossed into air like waves of gigantic horses rearing in the sun.

'Probably a good thing you didn't bring your wife,' the doctor said. 'It's bound to stink a bit down there.'

The doctor, an American, had a long face of loose indiarubber flesh, with shaggy brown eyebrows and a kindliness of demeanour that was also preoccupied. Our friendship sprang from the fact that I had helped him to look after a parcel of bugs as we came to Tahiti, across the Pacific, by seaplane. These bugs were larvae of a very large mosquito, an African species of cannibalistic habits that preyed on other mosquitoes, and it was the doctor's hope that presently they would also begin to prey on the mosquitoes of Tahiti.

'And will that help the elephantiasis?' I said.

'It might do. It's a chance,' he said. 'I believe in taking all the chances.'

When we got out of the car, some time later, the road had narrowed to a track of hot grey dust in the sun. Under the palms lay many fallen coconuts, each a green football with a hole in it, neatly bored.

'It is an interesting cycle,' the doctor said. We paused in the scalding sun and looked at the many punctured coconuts. 'The rat climbs the coconut palm and eats a hole in the coconut. The coconut falls and rain fills the hole with water. Mosquitoes breed in the water and fly off and bite an elephantiasis subject. Then they fly off again and bite someone who is not an elephantiasis subject but who, thanks to the mosquito, very soon will be.'

We began walking along a narrow path bordered on both sides by hedges of orange and crimson hibiscus, overlaid here and there with allamanda creepers bearing the softest yellow bells. At one place the flowers grew high enough to flash with brilliance against the far tossing white waves of the coral reef and suddenly sea, palms and flowers looked enchanting in the sun.

'The island is really very beautiful,' I said.

'An absolute lotus land.'

Presently there were no flowers: only occasional ragged banana trees and dusty bronze and yellow crotons with panting dogs lying in the dust beneath them.

'There are so many damned paths down here,' the doctor said, 'I'm never sure of the right one.'

Wooden shacks roofed mostly with palm frond but occasionally with pink corrugated iron began to appear everywhere under the coconut palms.

'This is it,' the doctor said. 'I always remember because of the bridge.'

The bridge was a single plank leading over an oozing grey-brown sewage gutter.

I followed the doctor across it and called: 'Who are you going to see here, doctor? Tahitians or Chinese?'

'Chinese,' he said. 'I'm going to try to get a man to take his pills.'

We were sitting, presently, in the compound of a wooden house in which there were several shallow water tanks. In the tanks three Chinese, two men and a woman, were washing vegetables. The woman was trimming spinach. When she had trimmed the spinach she dropped it into the tank and then paddled her bare feet in the water. The men paddled their feet in other tanks, one filled with watercress, the other with lettuces.

'I've always heard the Chinese were good at vegetables,' I began to say.

'*Institut Filariasis*,' the doctor said.

He said this loudly, several times, addressing the Chinaman who was paddling his feet in watercress. The man wore a pair of shorts the colour of an oil-rag from a garage but was otherwise naked except for a flat straw hat.

He grinned several times and nodded, showing the remains

of three yellow teeth in a mouth that was so thin and so fleshless that it looked almost skeletonized.

'*Institut Filariasis*,' the doctor said.

He said it several times in French, and then in English, in a strong American accent, as if he hoped that this would serve him better.

The Chinaman nodded impassively, paddling in watercress.

'Pills,' the doctor said. He said that too in French and then, more emphatically, in English.

The Chinaman paddled water and stared.

'He's promised to take the pills fifteen times already,' the doctor said to me. 'Last week he promised to take them today.'

The doctor took out of his trouser pocket a bottle of white capsules and began to unscrew the stopper. Seeing the capsule, the Chinaman, in a sort of pidgin French, began speaking very quickly. He stopped paddling his feet and made several gestures with skinny hands towards the sea. All the time the doctor sat watching him with a sort of ponderous sadness.

'What does he say?' I said.

'He is afraid to take the pills because he is fishing tonight. He says the pills will make him sick and he will faint and fall overboard.' He raised his voice and spoke in French to the Chinaman.

'The pills will not make you sick!'

The Chinaman let his mouth fall open, scratching his ribs at the same time.

'It is impossible for the pills to make you sick so that you will fall overboard,' the doctor said.

From out of the spinach tank the woman padded across the dust and hen-droppings of the compound to fetch, from under a tree, another basket of leaves. As she came back, tipped the spinach into the tank and paddled her feet in it once more I had a sudden impression, deep in my throat, that the steaming air had sickened.

'Look,' the doctor said. He poured two capsules into the palm of his hand and held them up to the Chinaman. 'Take them now. They will not make you sick. Let me see you take them now.'

The Chinaman stood up to his calves in watercress, staring,

and did not move. By the tap above the tank stood a cup. The doctor picked it up, turned on the tap and filled the cup with water. Then he held out the capsules in one hand and the cup in the other.

'It is very important,' he said in French. 'It is impossible for me to go until you take them.'

The Chinaman said something very quickly again.

'What does he say?'

'He says the big chief over at Bora-Bora wouldn't take them and if the chief is not obliged to take them why should he?'

'Is that right?'

'Unfortunately.'

His face was sweating now. His pouched indiarubber skin had flagged a little under the scalding sun. His air of slightly sad and preoccupied patience had left him for a moment and now he snapped at the Chinaman with a dozen cryptic words.

A moment later the Chinaman had the capsules in his hands. Then before putting them into his mouth he took the cup of water, drank it quickly and then filled it up again. The tortured skeleton of his face sucked at the water greedily and then suddenly he threw back his head and took the pills.

From the spinach tank the woman, in the high-pitched Chinese way, began laughing. The other man began laughing too, splashing water over his arms and calves at the same time. The Chinaman with the pills in his mouth stood for a moment impassively watching and then, filling and re-filling the cup, began swilling his mouth with water.

The woman with her high-pitched voice began giggling again and then took up, from beside the tank, a tin kettle, speaking for the first time to the doctor, who turned to me.

'They wish us to have tea,' he said. 'Would you care to have tea?'

'Would you?'

'I have to get out,' the doctor said.

The air was full of a smell of thickening hot decay. We shook hands with the three Chinese and said good-bye several times, first in French and then in English. The man and the woman who had not taken the pills stood respectively in lettuce and spinach, grinning. The man who had taken the pills looked at us with implacid downcast eyes.

At the top of the path, where air moved more freely among the tall palms, the hibiscus and the yellow creeper bells, I said to the doctor:

'Well, that was a win for you. You triumphed there.'

'He was holding them under his tongue all the time,' he said, 'the way they always do.'

Two minutes later we were driving along the black shining road beneath the palms. By the roadside there were many hedges of hibiscus and sometimes in the gardens tall forests of ginger-lily, like stiff gigantic ears of crimson corn.

As we drove along the doctor put his head out of the window and drank in deep draughts of cooler, rushing air.

'Well,' he said. 'This is Tahiti.' He drew in his head at last and waved one arm expressively, with slight sadness, towards the palms. 'What will you tell them when you get back?'

I looked beyond the palms and the black sand of the shore to where, far out, waves were bursting on the reef like the gigantic manes of thundering snow-white horses.

'I shall tell them,' I said, 'about the lotus land.'

FOR THE BEST IN PAPERBACKS, LOOK FOR THE ⓟ

In every corner of the world, on every subject under the sun, Penguin represents quality and variety – the very best in publishing today.

For complete information about books available from Penguin – including Pelicans, Puffins, Peregrines and Penguin Classics – and how to order them, write to us at the appropriate address below. Please note that for copyright reasons the selection of books varies from country to country.

In the United Kingdom: Please write to *Dept E.P., Penguin Books Ltd, Harmondsworth, Middlesex, UB7 0DA*

In the United States: Please write to *Dept BA, Penguin, 299 Murray Hill Parkway, East Rutherford, New Jersey 07073*

In Canada: Please write to *Penguin Books Canada Ltd, 2801 John Street, Markham, Ontario L3R 1B4*

In Australia: Please write to the *Marketing Department, Penguin Books Australia Ltd, P.O. Box 257, Ringwood, Victoria 3134*

In New Zealand: Please write to the *Marketing Department, Penguin Books (NZ) Ltd, Private Bag, Takapuna, Auckland 9*

In India: Please write to *Penguin Overseas Ltd, 706 Eros Apartments, 56 Nehru Place, New Delhi, 110019*

In Holland: Please write to *Penguin Books Nederland B.V., Postbus 195, NL–1380AD Weesp, Netherlands*

In Germany: Please write to *Penguin Books Ltd, Friedrichstrasse 10–12, D–6000 Frankfurt Main 1, Federal Republic of Germany*

In Spain: Please write to *Longman Penguin España, Calle San Nicolas 15, E–28013 Madrid, Spain*

In France: Please write to *Penguin Books Ltd, 39 Rue de Montmorency, F–75003, Paris, France*

In Japan: Please write to *Longman Penguin Japan Co Ltd, Yamaguchi Building, 2–12–9 Kanda Jimbocho, Chiyoda-Ku, Tokyo 101, Japan*

BY THE SAME AUTHOR

H. E. Bates

was one of the most popular and best-loved novelists of recent years. The following are some of the novels and stories published in Penguin.

The Triple Echo

H. E. Bates tells movingly the strange tale of a lonely woman and her love affair with a young deserter, of their intrigues and their deceptions and the elaborate web they weave to outwit the Military Police.

The Four Beauties

Four novellas, *The Simple Life*; *The Four Beauties*; *The Chords of Youth*; *The White Wind*, that reveal Bates's knowledge of human relationships.

Seven by Five

Subtle, passionate, tantalizing and direct, H. E. Bates explores the English character and scene from the mnid-twenties to the early sixties. This collection of stories bears witness to his claim to be master of the English short story.

Fair Stood the Wind for France

'*Fair Stood the Wind for France* is perhaps the finest novel of the war . . . The scenes are exquisitely done and the characters – tenderly and beautifully drawn – are an epitome of all that is best in the youth of the two countries. This is a fine, lovely book which makes the heart beat with pride' – *Daily Telegraph*

The Wild Cherry Tree

These ten stories show Bates at his most tense and immediate, observing with baleful accuracy just what happens when people are 'thrown suddenly with neither direction nor compass into territory utterly strange and unexplored'.

Love for Lydia

'Bates at his best . . . I read the tale with a sense of eager dread, so real are these folk, so torn and buffeted, and finally so humbled under the winds of passion and the even more terrifying peace which comes when the storm is over . . . A book likely to be one of the most-read love stories of our time' – Richard Church

The Purple Plain

The aircraft crashed miles from help in the Burmese wilderness. Assailed by heat, thirst and pain, three men set off on the long trek towards safety. 'It haunts you, alike for the queer and mounting suspense and for the masterly portraits of the three men' – *Sunday Times*

The Scarlet Sword

Kashmir, 1947. Partition has provoked political crisis and the fierce Pathans and Afridi of northern India come sweeping down from the hills to take part in the riot and massacre.
A small Catholic mission is in their path, and for ten days its inhabitants suffer the nightmare of murderous attack and occupation.